Dearest Kat

GARGANTUA NOW

RABELAISE

"A ROLLICKING RABELAISIAN COMEDY - NEVER KNEW SHE COULD BE SO FUNNY!"

Allmy Bestfriends

I so hope you enjoy this!

with love —

Rob x

First published by O Books, 2007
O Books is an imprint of John Hunt Publishing Ltd.,
The Bothy, Deershot Lodge, Park Lane, Ropley, Hants, SO24 0BE, UK
office1@o-books.net
www.o-books.net

Distribution in:

UK and Europe
Orca Book Services
orders@orcabookservices.co.uk
Tel: 01202 665432 Fax: 01202 666219 Int. code (44)

USA and Canada
NBN
custserv@nbnbooks.com
Tel: 1 800 462 6420 Fax: 1 800 338 4550

Australia and New Zealand
Brumby Books
sales@brumbybooks.com.au
Tel: 61 3 9761 5535 Fax: 61 3 9761 7095

Far East (offices in Singapore, Thailand, Hong Kong, Taiwan)
Pansing Distribution Pte Ltd
kemal@pansing.com
Tel: 65 6319 9939 Fax: 65 6462 5761

South Africa
Alternative Books
altbook@peterhyde.co.za
Tel: 021 447 5300 Fax: 021 447 1430

Design: Stuart Davies

ISBN-13: 978 1 84694 059 0
ISBN-10: 1 84694 059 1

A CIP catalogue record for this book is available from the British Library.

Printed in Great Britian by Ashford Colour Press Ltd

GARGANTUA NOW

RABELAISE

Winchester, UK
Washington, USA

This book is dedicated

To Gargantua

As always, the helpful in this book comes from you, the unhelpful from me.

This is your copyright.

To my children, Oliver, India and Caspar for your criticism, support, patience, listening and ideas. Thank you for putting up with me. I love you very much.

Contents

CHAPTER ONE

OF PREGNANCY AND THE BIRTH OF THE MOST REMARKABLE GARGANTUA

Pantagruel and Bigfortydeedee's union was one of deep love, marred only by the lack of a child. The doctors were perplexed as to the best way forward since Bigfortydeedee was, in spite of modern medical advances, a little past child bearing age. Consultant after consultant fed her special treatments, including one hundred and fourteen attempts at in vitro fertilisation. She saw healers, homeopaths, acupuncturists. She put up pictures of babies in favoured feng-shui places. She did the usual abstaining to stop worrying about it (to Pantagruel's discomfiture) and even had prayers said by monks.

Nobody really knew who or what was responsible but finally, when Bigfortydeedee was six hundred and sixty nine, she became pregnant. Pantagruel put it down to a particular position but for whatever reason, they were both delighted. Scans ensued allowing the most beautiful sightings in vitro. The parents-to-be were enthralled oohing and aahing at their future son, already playing with his dingleby-dangleby. 'Just like his father' Bigfortydeedee laughed.

'I want a water birth' she insisted.

'But darling, it's a little impractical' Pantagruel gently

countered to no avail. A pregnant giantess was known to have a rather strong will.

'I'll do it in public' Bigfortydeedee cried. 'I'll do it for charity. Book of records. After all, it will be the first giant born in several hundred years'.

Pantagruel demurred muttering that dictum belonging to all time and all creeds, giantesses included, under his breath: *'it is a woman's prerogative to change her mind'*.

Monitoring the child's heartbeat was no mean feat either. Midwives had to climb on a ladder to reach the womb and listen with specially made horns. But the foetus would make so much noise gargling that the midwife's hearing would soon go for a Burton. So it was only a few devoted experts (among them Dartagne, more in chapter seven) and pioneers in the field who would take the risk.

It took five hundred workmen sixteen weeks to build the bathtub but then Bigfortydeedee cried for days insisting she had made a mistake and would prefer to give birth in a clinic in the USA.

'But you can't possibly fly now, dear' Pantagruel tried to talk sense.

'No, but I could walk' she exclaimed with wild determination.

Pantagruel tried to keep hush-hush.

Luckily she changed her mind at the last minute, developing a preference for nesting in her natural habitat where evi-odent-ly birth could be performed au naturel. Their current home was a private forest called Singwolf on the top of a secluded hill in the middle of the countryside. It was the perfect location.

Her EDD had arrived, by GMT standard time of four hundred weeks' gestation. The French insisted four hundred and ten weeks was correct. To induce or not to induce? To plan a Caesarean, to stave off the inconvenience of pain or go for the push?

Meanwhile, Pantagruel developed a case of prenatal nerves. He made himself useful by checking the taps which would fill the bathtub. It mustn't be too hot and it mustn't be too cold. He checked the appropriate music and sound system were functioning properly. Bigfortydeedee was adamant that she must have the right ambiance and had selected her favourite music to encourage peaceful labour:

The Charge of the Light Brigade
The flight of the Bumblebees
Scottish bagpipes
Hoomi singers
Wagner
India ragas
Led Zeppelin
Frank Zappa
Disney favourites
Stranger in the night
Puff the magic dragon

As back-up she had a collection of four thousand CDs.

'Was that enough?' Pantagruel worried.

He checked the lighting. Natural lighting was a must. They

had bought five hundred thousand night lights. Good thing he checked because he had forgotten to buy matches. He rushed to the corner shop for an ample supply.

By the side of the tub lay a few thousand oranges to soothe his wife's thirst if she felt so inclined. He hoped they wouldn't be overripe by the time labour started.

There could be no doubt: all the practical considerations were taken care of. Time seemed to go on forever with the couple getting more and more wound up. Bigfortydeedee ate four thousand curries. Pantagruel exceeded himself and they made love 120 times that night. To no avail.

Even the imperturbable Dartagne showed a chink: he coughed. Just once. Maybe he should encourage hospitalisation.

The only solution was to watch DVDs.

Bigfortydeedee insisted on 'Gone with the wind', winding herself up more and more as she watched Scarlett deliver a baby in blazing fire. It looked painful. After the hundred and tenth viewing, Pantagruel insisted. "Forty Towels' or we make love again'. Much as she loved him, the thought of making love again was a little too taxing, so she conceded.

It worked. Comedy did the trick. She laughed and laughed and laughed so much until suddenly a sharp pain made her double over.

'That's it!' she screamed jubilantly. 'the baby's a coming'. The nurses and Dartagne were over in a jiffy checking her pulse and the baby's heartbeat. 'We recommend you don't jump in the bath immediately because it will delay the proceedings'. Bigfortydeedee agreed wholeheartedly but still climbed straight in.

Pantagruel was the perfect new man. He kept the heat at the right temperature and fed her oranges one by one.

'*Please* peel them' she reminded him as he placed a whole one in her mouth.

The tempo rose. Her breathing sharpened. The moment approached.

'Beethoven's ninth, Beethoven's ninth' Bigfortydeedee yelled. Pantagruel rushed for the collection and put it on.

'Baa baa black sheep, have you any wool?' sounded out.

Bigfortydeedee was so startled that she gave a final push and out came their baby giant in all his glory.

'And one for the little boy who lives down the lane'.

'Turn that silly music off' she yelled to an exhausted Pantagruel.

'That was such hard work' he exclaimed and fell into a faint.

Dartagne handed Bigfortydeedee her baby.

And so Gargantua was born.

CHAPTER TWO

Of the origins of the great Gargantua

It would be fitting, since we all have so much spare time on our hands nowadays with all our modern machinery, to briefly tell of the origins of Gargantua. All great chronicles start in such a way and it would not do to change the form.

A short while ago, at the beginning of this particular world, forty times forty nights ago at least, after the period when the Greeks were the masterminds, before the Arab and Latin empire, just after the British, (I must be precise so you cannot fail to recognize it), after the particularly noticeable period when *the Empire* who thought it was so very invincible and everlasting, was ruling the world, there was a huge earthquake. Earthquake Darveda. Gushes of sea spilled forth, ejaculating from the Atlantic and Adriatic and Pacific and Specific into the New Rift and the skies blazed furiously emitting more than the usual angry venom of black clouds and torrential rain. *Visit Michelangelo's website.*

Starry, starry night. A full moon. It was the equinox. Of course. Everyone was asleep but a dog looked upwards and saw. The kaleidoscopic dream. He saw the great emptiness, the great clouds and gases, the millions of galaxies, the fiery stars, the rain, meteorites, torrents, asteroids, comets and amidst it all, a big and beautiful **SOAP BUBBLE.**

Time stopped.

The soap bubble begat bacteria and algae. They begat shells, jellyfish, corals and seaplants. They begat millipedes, worms and insects. They begat frogs and salamanders. They begat dinosaurs. The dinosaurs begat giants but both were wiped out by another earthquake allowing the crocodiles, birds and mammals to beget apes. The apes begat homo sapiens and our old friends, Adam and Eve. They were considered leaders in their field and of the best peerage. Unbeknownst to Adam however, Eve had had a dream and in this dream had consummated wild union with a giant who had exploded into her bed from a cannon which had been set off at a circus performance on the very day dinosaurs and giants had been wiped from earth. It was a genome in a million and, by all accounts, a love-making session in a trillion, from which a highly successful secret breed ensued. The first was Giantooth who begat Mazeltoff (a great matchmaker) who begat Molotov (who invented the finest cocktail), who begat Bestov, which began the fashion for double-barrelled names, who begat Bestov-Worstov, who begat Rockon-Rockov who begat and changed his name to Rollov-Beethov (a great musician) who begat Rollon-Beatov (creator of a most sensuous deodorant) who begat Milou-Ranov (a frightened dog-like giant), who begat Tintin Forrall (a travelling hero) who decided to go back to his roots and do away with double-barrelled mania. He begat Pantagruel who married Bigfortydeedee when she was five hundred and forty nine years old. With a little effort they begat Gargantua.

CHAPTER 3

OF THE MISSING OF THE MOMENT, CLOUDS, FACTS AND ODES

Of course, Pantagruel and Bigfortydeedee had tried to keep the birth a small low-key occasion. Luckily, it coincided with an eagerly awaited moment. The world was on to 'it'. The thing was, nobody knew what 'it' would be but everyone knew something marvellous was about to happen.

The world thought it was a new beginning. A fresh start. A renaissance, even. Scientists had proved and disproved and approved and reproved the Big Bang Theory and thought the world might tip into a new abyss. Everyone who knew wanted to have veni, vidi, vici, not just Caesar. Everyone who knew wanted to behold the new beginning, the dawn of a new era, beyond the age of Aquarius. Actresses uncovered their breasts on stage the world over.

'Don't watch without special sunglasses!' television warned.

'Don't look headlong!' radio blared.

'Don't let the sky fall on your head!' Asterix yelled to Obelix.

Astrologers had been ready of course. They reckoned it was all to do with the recently discovered planet Chichi affecting the cloaked and invisible planet Potter, known to be there but seen by none. Prediction magazines had heralded:

-'THE CHICHI CHOP'-

A day when all fifteen planets would be opposite each other in detriment in the world house, following the Kushy system. Pluto would bark, Venus go frigid and Mars attack, and Neptune would delude which would cause the Sun to be severely distressed and out of position, in disposition and indisposed.

Unfortunately, owing to an error in their hard drive, they had got the date wrong. As had the majority of the Western world, who owing to another computer glitch, were using the Chinese calendar system and forming 'the year of twenty months', with three Augusts to increase the sale of suntan lotion.

It was still a starry, starry night. Don McLain and revellers still danced at Stonehenge. Desert fish popped out of the sand by the thousand. Nudists marked the moment by flocking to their camps and making merry. Americans listened to Oprah Winfrey. Mystics muttered mantras. The global net kept all informed.

These are indeed important facts for you to know. Historians and fat controllers would be nowhere without these details. Collectible facts. Memorabilia. History to be. Precision. Two plus two equal four. The president did not make love to his mistress. Marilyn Monroe was not assassinated. Marlowe was a spy. D Day did happen. The earth is not flat. Anastasia did not survive. DNA proof. Man has travelled to the moon. We do not have evidence of beings from out of space. Leonardo was not right, people would not fly.

So, therefore, dear readers, I am sure you want to know the precise moment of this world changing event. The moment. The moment in time (never!). That moment.

Even the poet laureate had been commissioned to write the last word on the moment but....

The fact was,

....

the moment

was...nononononononono..........................oh

oh........

missed.

All the bard could do was write a tragic ode:

'Not a starry but a dark night
Please do shed a little light
On our mightily troubled plight:
For indeed, we've lost our sight.
No, we weren't caught in a tryst.
Nor were we sealed with a loving kiss.
It was because of the foggy mist
That, lamentably, 'the moment was missed'

Clouds blew over *the moment* at that very *moment* to such an extent that *the moment* was not seen or experienced in the *moment*. It only took a *moment* for everyone to miss 'it'.

In despair, the six lines became a national refrain and then a global one, called '*The missing of the moment*'.

Copyrights were forcibly honoured. Everyone was singing it. The Chinese tried to interpret its deep meaning. It was considered as important an ode as Mao's Little Red Book. 'Dallas' changed their theme tune to the refrain. Whilst the Scots played a marvellous version on the bagpipes.

Radio and television reporters the world over reported the non-event in the grandest of detail.

After the discovery of the wheel, the '*missing of the moment*' became the greatest event in history.

And so, by complete chance, it came to be that Gargantua was born in peace. Nobody knew of his appearance, nor could they put their finger on the magic change in the world.

But it didn't take long for things to change. Indeed, since things do inevitably change, it was impossible for labels not to rear their head.

CHAPTER FOUR

OF GARGANTUA'S LABELS, BREAST MILK, BATTERIES AND HALF A SIXPENCE

Ah yes, labels. Sixty seconds starting from now.

LABELS

SABEL, SABLE, BALES, SBEAL, BLESAL, LEBLAS.

You know those labels: from the moment you were born, people stuck labels in your mouth. And Gargantua, giant or not, was no exception.

Imagine your mouth as a front door. Everyone posting labels through your letterbox. Well, this was Gargantua's lot as well.

OPEN WIDE, dear, just a little more down the letterbox.

Just a spoonful of sugar. Glug glug.

And before he knew it, he had swallowed the labels. They churned around in his stomach.

Dummy,

Big nipple label,

Heinz fruit puree label,

Nettles baby powder milk ('let's sting the natural way')

fresh mother's milk mixed with curry,

tea,

a dash of earth from his mother's fingernail,

a blob of perfume,

polluted air,

half a sixpence,

anti-allergenic specks of pillow dust particles,

daddy's spit,

three flies,

a random ant,

the foam letter A off a floating mobile which accidentally dropped into his mouth.

Need I carry on?

Clearly, even giants could not avoid it: the moment they started breathing, they started dying a little. Oh what a wonderful life. Oh what a beautiful feeling, oh what a wonderful day. I am sure **none** of you have ever doubted it. Or have you?

It *is* a wonderful life. I am telling you, according to edict 10564 of the millennium directory. Look around you. The Hills are alive with the sound of music. Da da da da.

And that was only his mouth.

What about his ears? No, what about anyone's ears?

Cars zooming back and forth. Rrrrrrrrrrrrrrrr. Rrrrrrrrrrrrrrrrrrrrrr.

Drunken yobs yelling. Bif bof. Bash.

Beethoven. Tatatatam.

BBC world service. ‘*This is Prissy Perfect with wailing world wobbles at four*’.

The Archers. Dadadadadadada.

Neighbours. Neieieieieieieghbours.

Yelling. YOU ––-YOU––YOU––

Parents’ lovemaking. Or maybe not. .... Noisy Silence.

Beloved sibling’s mantra whispered when parents-aren’t-looking: ‘Go back where you came from’, ‘Go back where you came from’. ‘They don’t want you, they want me’, ‘they don’t want you, they want me’.

In Gargantua’s case it was the nursery rhyme.

Twinkle twinkle little star. Twinkle twinkle little star. Twinkle twinkle little star. Twiiiiiiiiiiiiiiiikkkkkkkkkkeeeeeeeeeeeeeeeeeeeeeeeel twiiiii-iiiiiiiiiiiiiiiiiiikkkkkkkkkkkkkkkkkkkkkkkkkkkkkkkellllllllllll-l l l l l l l l l l l l l l l l l l littttttttttttttttttttttttttttttttttttttttttttttttttle ssssssssssssstaaaaaaaaaaaaaaaaaaaaaaaaaaaaarrrr:

The musical toy above his cot intoned again and agaiiiiiiiii-iiiiinnnnn.

(‘*If I hear that once more, I’ll vaporise and disappear’, he tried to think, learning to punch his giant little hands in the air and kick his tiny huge legs)*

And finally it came out:

‘B-b-b-batteries’.

His first completely formed thought.

‘Get some new batteries, Mummy!’

A little anger had erupted.

Oh no! Gargantua farted loudly.

Mummy rushed in and changed the music to whale sounds. Whooooooooooo oooooohhhhhh, whaaaaaaaaaaaaaaaaaaaaahhhhhhhhhhhhhhhhh, whoooooooooooooooooooooooo, whhhhhhhhhh-haaaaaaaaaaaaaaaaaaaahhhhhhh.

('I'm not a whale, Mummy, please give me a break' he cried).

Feeling dizzy, he burped.

'*Ooohh, well done. You'll feel better now, darling*' his parents gushed.

Only a few days' old and yet the labels had 'got him'.

The world had got him, under its skin. It had got him, deep in the heart of it. Or he had got the world under his skin. His letterbox was already full. What to do?

CHAPTER FIVE

OF GROWING, PINTS, GSTRINGS AND VEGGY

There was only one thing he could do. Grow. And grow he did. Rapidly and enormously. Gargantua was doing marvellously but Bigfortydeedee was getting tired.

It had been impossible to hire a maternity nurse willing to take on such a giant task so that in spite of plentiful nannies busying themselves with nappies at the ready and the constant washing and ironing of giant-tiny sailor suits, Bigfortydeedee was succumbing to the extra weight. She was now EnormousSixtygeegee and could hardly move for the added pressure.

Pantagruel, recovered from the exertions of labour, tried helplessly to hold her up as she moved around. She misinterpreted his motivation and shrugged him off. Fed up, he let her be and went off to drown his solace at the local pub. Over a large number of pints of beer, he discovered he was not alone.

'She just won't let me come near her' he cried.

'I know, I know' the men grunted into their froth without looking up. Another man continued.

'I mean, I was given a hunting bonus the other day and gave it to my wife -the most beautiful fox collar-it was and she started yelling at me' Jack said.

'I know, I know' the men grunted into their froth.

'Don't tell me she's gone veggie like my Maggie?' Joe asked.

'Does she tell you you can't eat meat no more 'cos you don't know what's innit?'

'Absolutely. Spot on. Exactly that. Only plate after plate of veg. No fish either.'

'I know, I know' the men grunted into their froth.

'But not only that. I have to go home and cook now. I mean, I mean. I'm a man. My mother always cooked for my dad and now **I've** got to cook. And not even a barbecue.' John groaned.

'I know, I know' the men grunted into their froth.

'I know she means well but it's all to do with health. On and on like. Nag, nag, nag. '*Think of that poor animal, George, think of it being slaughtered. Look at all the blood on your plate, George. Don't know where it's been, do you? Think of all the additives, George. ADD, BSD, RSJ, full fat cream, SAD, ABC. And what was the latest one? OTT, was it? Think of all the suffering they've been through, George.*'

And then, I'm about to put the most delicious bit of fillet steak into my mouth, and she just looks at me, just looks at me in that certain way and starts to cry. '*Think how that cow must have been so scared. So scared, all his life, waiting for the moment when he'd be slaughtered. And the butchering carries on because people like you* ***ENJOY, ENJOY*** *putting bits of his organs in your mouth. I mean, would you eat its balls? I know some people do, but would you? It's an animal, just like you and me. Just think of that, George, think of that. Are you listening, dear? Think of that, I could be eating our little Johnny. Or worse, his balls. Not much different is it?*' Nag,

nag, nag.' George went on .

'I know, I know' the men grunted into their froth.

'Well, my wife, like, well, she comes home and yells to me, like: '*Darling, have you ironed my blue silk shirt for tonight? We're late already. It was that board meeting. I had to be there of course. Sort out the junior secretaries: they were out of hand. I don't know what it is with young men today but they graduate, get a job as a secretary and immediately want* **my** *job! Boy, I'm knackered. Don't suppose you managed to get a shop at Sadways?'* She completely ignores how I'm feeling and just puts her feet up while I get on with the cleaning. Otherwise, the house would be a tip. She doesn't seem to notice the mess and I can't stand it. Lipstick everywhere. Bras all over the floor. G strings under the sofa. She never bothers to pick up a thing. I've even gone off knickers. G strings mean cleaning to me, not fun anymore.' Jim complained.

'I know, I know' the men grunted into their froth.

'But not only that. You can't even complain because they earn more than we do. My Maggie went out and bought a bright pink people carrier without even asking me. Just like that. I have no control. It weren't like that when I were young. Dad earnt the money and Mum had a jar she kept her housekeeping in. He made all the important decisions. Didn't matter whether she liked it or not. And they were happy. Lovely meals every night on the table, clean home and perfectly laundered shirts, sheets and sex. Idyllic.' John moaned.

'I know, I know, the men grunted into their froth.'

'But not only that. When my Angie gets 'ome, she goes for a lie-down while I do the kids. So by the time 8pm comes around, I just crawl into bed and fall straight asleep. And then she's got 'er 'ands all over me. All over. And she won't let go. That's all she wants: nookey and more nookey. And not just satisfied with the basic stuff. She wants *sophistication*. Don't know where she gets it from. Must be all those dirty mags she reads on the bus. The one with all those nude men with huge plonkers. Know what I mean?'

'Yes, yes, yes. And not only that. I pretend to be asleep but I guarantee the missus will turn up in some new negligee and try and seduce me. Every night. And it's getting worse. *Every night*. I ask you.'

'I know, I know' the men grunted into their froth.

They bought another round of drinks.

They smoked more cigarettes.

They looked at the huge television screen on the wall.

'What's the football score?' Pantagruel asked.

'No football tonight, guv, it's not the season. That's why they're all so maudlin' the landlord explained.

'They can cope with everything when the football's on. They drink the sherry tucked in their kitchen cupboards and then they come in here and blot it all out.'

Pantagruel had come from another world but now he thought he might be about to find out what sterner men were made of. Was this truly man's lot? Was bromide truly rampant in the rivers? Were men really losing their reproductive ability? Was this causing the advent of 'Man United'? No, cross that out and change to 'Manhood disenchanted'?

'Don't look so worried, mate, have another pint' one of the

lads interrupted his thoughts.

Pantagruel fancied he could hear Gargantua crying.

'No, I'd better go home now'.

'Well, good luck, mate and you know where to find us. Mens' sorority and all that. We jolly well need to stick together now. Cup of tea and listening ear always available.'

CHAPTER SIX

OF NURSERY, HEALTH AND SAFETY, LICE AND FIRST WORDS

Bigfortydeedee was in a quandary as to which nursery to choose for Gargantua. She listened to other mothers recommending the 'Brightest Kids' Academy', the 'Read-at-three-months nursery', the 'Einstein-at-two' playgroup and the 'nursery-that-anyone-who-is-anyone-just-must-send-their-kids-to' and those that were 'so-very-exclusive-unless- you-had- put- his- name- down- before- he- was -even- a- thought -and- before- you- had -even- heard- of- them'.

She had a look around some, checking on the physical advantages: wired fences to keep out potential pervs, covered-up ponds to stop the babies falling in, hard lino floors to prevent childrens' allergies to wool, one hundred individual washbasins to stop the children spreading germs. This naturally took up space in the playroom.

The only inscriptions on the wall were huge lists:

HEALTH AND SAFETY COUNCIL RULES

All children who enter must have a face, two legs and one mouth.

All children must have three hundred spare pants.

All children must be protected from breathing outside air

for cause of pollution.
All children must be protected from breathing inside air, for cause of infection.
All children must avoid eating chips, baked beans, sugar and spice and anything nice for fear of e-coli.
All children must therefore avoid eating.
(The above had been crossed out as being an amendment to the childrens' act of 1885, '*asking for more*' would henceforth be forbidden for fear of Dickensian reprisals)
All children must refrain from putting paintings on the walls for fear of one accidentally falling down on their head.
All children must stand still to avoid accidents.
All children forbidden from touching each other at any point for fear of accusations of bullying.
All children must report to a senior in charge if any member of staff should accidentally touch them.
(approved by the SimonSays government health and safety department section 2005BCAD)

Whenever Bigfortydeedee asked for explanations as to why the children could not move, the principals of each and every established establishment shuddered and shook, a wild look in their eyes and uttered the only words:

'The rules, the rules, the rules. It's the rules.'

One of them even broke down in tears and fell into her arms, sobbing uncontrollably.

'The rules, the rules, they keep on changing the rules. I see rules, implement, make rules, dream rules but God forbid that

I should break rules.' Remarkably coincidentally, she had a large, rather nasty looking ruler in her hands.

Back at home, only two days later, Bigfortydeedee found herself scratching her head on an almost constant basis.

Dartagne, on his weekly round, noticed immediately:

'You've got lice'.

'I beg your pardon' she questioned.

'Can't be anything else. You must have come into contact with some other infected kids. It's uncontrollable these days. I'll get you a lice comb.'

That decided her. Nursery was out of the question. Absolutely out of the question. Pantagruel, of the most affable disposition, concurred.

Gargantua was no ordinary child anyway. He shocked everyone by being able to speak on day seven. He had no need for precocious nurseries for Norms. His mother's breasts sufficed.

His first formed thought became his first spoken sentence:

'Batteries, mum, get some new batteries'.

Bigfortydeedee was startled but so delighted with her son's genius that she complied immediately.

On day fourteen, he could be found carving the word 'batteries' into a large rock and it was so doing that he made rather an important meeting.

In England, there was a young lady from the village Behind who had a rather large backside. One morning she lay asleep in bed, hugging her beautiful silk sheets and had a dream.

In her dream, she thought she was holding a man.

A nice hunk of a man.

Shall we give him a name? Why? Just another label.

So she had a week of a dream and woke up.

These words came upon her.

'You know you have to decide.

You can no longer hide.

Go, be taken from Behind'.

So

With only a small bag, travelling light

She took a new cheap airline flight

That landed her in cloudy sight

Of Singwolf and Giant Might

Not knowing if she were still alive

She carved her name on kriptonite

Scared lest she had erred too right

She fortified her label with araldite

She might have flown in light as a kite

But she did not want to be a dead mite.

Before day would become night

She would know: was she dead or knight?

Was she wrong or right?

'Batteries' Gargantua cried, hammering away at the rock.

'Zzorroa' She cried, etching into her kryptonite dolmen.

Gargantua turned round, startled.

'Sorrow?' he asked.

'No Zzorroa with an extra Z, diddle diddle diddle dum' she corrected.

'Ah, zo' he added. Gargantua had made his first friend.

CHAPTER SEVEN

OF ZZORROA, Z, ADDICTIONS, BIRDS, MSN AND BREASTS

'That's a nice name' Gargantua commented, speaking clearly and lucidly and eruditely and elocutionally and dramatically and profoundly.

'Thanks' ZZORROA replied. 'Did you know that the letter Z was created as the result of a soldier leaning too hard on his sword as he fell asleep? He had understood the secret of the universe and if you ever visit the world of 610 000 BC in your dreams, you will find Z's were etched in the rocks everywhere as people tried to emulate him. A magical man. Unfortunately, because the effect was sleep, there is no longer physical evidence of this society. Anyway, I'm ZZORROA with the extra Z. Diddle diddle diddle dumb'.

'I'm Gargantua, which means 'que grand tu as' but it got lost in translation. The name is meant to give me the confidence I need in life, along with my mother's breasts. My mother's called Bigfortydeedee.'

Meanwhile, back at home, Bigfortydeedee was suffering. She had fallen asleep on the sofa and was dreaming of birds sucking her nipples. She tried to shoo them away but a man called Hitchcock kept on sending fresh flocks of migrant voracious birds to her bedside. She woke up, her arms waving frantically in the air, shielding herself from a dejected Pantagruel who turned away from her. She was too tired to reach out and cuddle him anyway. The whole episode brought on her silent

Despairing lament for all new mothers

Oh, would she sleep through the night again?
Oh, would she ever be free?
Oh, would she have a brain again?
Oh, would she ever have energy?
Oh, would she be beautiful again?
Oh, would she ever be feminine?
Oh, would her breasts stop leaking again?
Oh, would she ever be trim?

Meanwhile Zzorroa was telling Gargantua more of the wonderful mystery of the letter Z.

'It's great, Gargantua. Archeologists recently uncovered the original sword. It's etched into stone in the shape of a Z. Try as they might, nobody can lift it out. It's rapidly becoming a landmark place to visit along with Madame Tussaud's, the CN Tower, Lourdes, The Wailing Wall, Lenin's tomb, Borobodur, Disneyland and the statue of Peter Pan. People troop by but because of the nature of the letter Z, they fall asleep. Insomniacs travel there in their millions, eager to find a cure. Bedrooms rentable by the hour have been set up with all profits going to the Z foundation. And the question remains: 'will anyone be able to lift out the sword?

Some serious adults have even become addicted to the 'Z high'. No different from

-children to coca-cola
-teenagers to jeans and trainers
-mobile users to their chargers
-television viewers to their soaps
-msn users to mesmerism or is it s&m, or m&s,
-popeye to his spinach
-builders to their cups of tea
-chairmen to their bonuses
-powermaniacs to their busy-ness
-sweet-toothers to their sugar
-fitness fanatics to their aerobics
-dogs to their bones
-pleasure seekers to unlimited sex
-music lovers to Ipods
-junkies to their fix
-victims to their woes
-cigarette smokers to their cigarettes (we mustn't of course mention brands such as Marlboro, Rothmans, Dunhill, Silkcut, Sobranie, Benson and Hedges, and a few more or we will get sued)

Gargantua listened fascinated, but addicted as he himself was to Bigfortydeedee's breasts (his comfortables, as he called them), he excused himself and walked home.

He found both his parents slumped on the sofa, merrily snoring away. Squeezing himself into a gap, he grasped his mother's breasts and had a copious drink.

THE ODE OF BABIES' HAPPINESS

Ah, the bliss of mother's comfortables

The taste of complete security
It unleashes inutterable
Paroxysms of bliss and delectability.
Squashed between two big breasts
Definitely makes for the very best.

Gargantua had all the good ingredients for a happy life: two parents who had been together for a long time, love, big bosoms, and no nursery. He had also made his first million:

'Squashed between two big breasts
Definitely makes for the very best.'

was to become the logo for the 'fight against tinned baby milk' campaign.

CHAPTER EIGHT

Of Zzorroa meeting Dartagne, public schools, nans, sausages and politics

Zzorroa had remained carving her dolmen. She was still not sure where she was but was trying to grapple with her new surroundings. Carving her initial gave her a sense of clinging to something she knew. Her name. Her label. Her identity. If anyone passed by they could trace her. She would have left her mark. She wouldn't have disappeared completely. Perhaps she should put her email down as well? But then she didn't have her laptop with her.

She was sure she was still alive. Indeed far more alive than at home. She didn't regret flying off into the unknown for a second - except that no meals were provided on her flight- but was a little worried about what to do next. And, along with other pressing matters, she needed the loo.

She looked quizzically at the word 'Batteries' etched into the rock and wondered about its hidden meaning. It was etched close to carvings of herds of bison. Did it mean electric cows?

At this very moment Dartagne rode by. As the reader might already have gathered, Dartagne was a very special doctor. It is not everyday that someone is called in to attend to the birth of a giant. But he had long been involved with the family.

He came from a long lineage of doctors and masters of fencing (his father having won the silver medal in the 1933 Olympics). As a boy, Dartagne had had the traditional upbringing, meant to offer the very best. Name put down before birth for Sgink, leading public school, and sent to boarding school at 4. Just like his father.

'Toughens you up, dear boy, toughens you up. I had to crack the ice in the bucket of water so I could wash in the morning and then run up and down a hill before breakfast. And look at me now'.

Pupils developed life-long- love affairs with their favourite teddy (Dartagne's was called Mr. Cuddles.) If ever you have wondered why teddy bear shops abound and teddy bears 'guaranteed genuine last-a-life-time' sell so well, look no further. Of course, some people had the same feelings for their railway sets, playing with them well into their dotage. Houses sold at higher prices if they contained a 'special bed for teddy' and 'your own exclusive toy train rail track spread over four floors'.

And some developed love, as Dartagne did, for their Nan. Or Nanny. Not nano. And some had it bad. Dartagne lost a part of himself forever when his nan left. A gram. Anagram. No more tears. No more nan. No more Pop ins. Mary and her brolly had popped off.

So Sgink was famed for tears being deleted from an early age. Cooked breakfasts were a must as the alternative. Sausages instead of tears. Hence the term: 'Now be a good sausage'.

When Dartagne asked the headmaster what the school

motto was the headmaster looked surprised and replied:

'The motto?'

'*Always look on the bright side of life*'.

Sorry, cross out and replace

'Whatever whenever however, venimus, vidimus, vicimus FAMILYIS ET GOVERNMENTIS floreatis'.

Cross out again.

'*We know which side our bread is buttered on*'

Cross out again.

'*Rule Britannia*'

Cross out again.

'*Old ties*'

Every time the headmaster spoke, his mouth would eject the words as his head flipped backwards. A bit like Zebedee or Jack in the Box. Poing, poing. Ping.

Dartagne had been brought up on status quo and good manners. After A******** grades in all his exams he was creamed into one of the few universities worth considering. Whisking his brain to a suitable pulp, they failed to notice his escape during a long summer vacation. Travelling in search of adventure, he rode through hill and dale, across mountains and sea until, in pouring rain, he bumped into a statue. The top of the statue accidentally fell off and knocked him unconscious. He lay there for goodness knows how long until he woke to someone feeding a cup of water to his lips. When he realized that the face looking at him was extremely large and that he was cradled in the breasts of a huge giantess his perceptions changed forever.

'I am Bigfortydeedee' she introduced herself.

'You bumped into an old family statue and knocked yourself out. Your horse ran off in terror. But do not fear. Fear kills. Trust and all will be well.'

Dartagne had no choice but to do as he was told and had remained with the family for the last few decades trying to understand what he had actually bumped into.

His mission?

Mission impossible.

He had three seconds to listen to his instructions before the tape would self-destruct.

= To understand the world of giants and so save the world. =

Easy really, as long as he had Mr. Cuddles by his side.

He would never walk alone.

In a hurry to visit Bigfortydeedee he caught sight of Zzorroa carving her name in the rock. As ever the dashing hero he enquired:

'Can I help you?'

Startled by the voice, Zzorroa turned around and caught sight of the dazzling doctor with the gleaming white teeth. The world stopped for her. Music rang in her ears.

He walked so slowly that she took photos in her mind of his every move. Left leg up, left leg down. Right leg forward, right leg up, right leg down. Knee straightened. Left leg up, left leg forward, left leg down. Slight pull on the stomach muscles. Chin up, mouth fractionally open. Hair blowing back. Left hand forward, swaying by his side. Right hand forward, swaying by his side. Left shoulder up, left shoulder down.

She asked, shyly but desperately:

'Do you know where the nearest restrooms are?'

She looked down at her feet, embarrassed.

There was nothing for it. Dartagne suggested she accompany him to SingWolf...

CHAPTER NINE

OF RESTROOMS, ATTRACTION, NOVEL WAYS, LOOS AND TINKLES

As they walked, Zzzorroa held extremely important philosophical debates inside her head about 'the right word'. Had she used the correct term? Should she have used

Loo
Lavatory
Ladies
Gents
Gentleman
Dames
Hommes
Messieurs
Toilettes
Los Servicios
Little boy's room
Thingemijig
Spend a penny
Bog (yuk!)
The you-know-what's-it
Where can I have a tinkle
Where can I have a pee
Urination point

Wet patch

Have a wee

The unisex facilities

The bathroom

The ???.... (for those too shy to actually use a word) (ah,yes, of course, first on the right)

The ...(index finger pointed upwards with a hopeful look in the eye)(ah yes, first on the left down the corridor, take the steps down, around the corner and straight ahead- you'll see the sign- you really can't miss it-)

She knew the world was in turmoil but seriously considered this dilemma to be one of the gravest problems to afflict mankind since the advent of lavatories. What did they ask for in olden days?

Did one enquire?

'Where is the garderobe, please? I have urgent needs to attend to.'

Did one check if outside were vacant? Not 'mind the gap' but 'mind the flying object.' Did one check the waste was allowed to fall to the ground in dead zones unimpeded?

But what to do today if your loo were taken away? You would rush unknowingly to your trusted spot and discover that the loo had disappeared. 'Sorry gov, gone on strike today'. And then what to do? Display calm and non-attachment? No, that wouldn't help the urgent situation. Jump up and down? No, that would make the condition worse. Count to ten? No, that would make the problem more desperate. Try and pretend all is illusion. No, that would lead to more wet patches. Go and scream at the neighbour that they were stealing seriously valuable property? No, they would be out at work or punch you. No community spirit left today.

She dared anyone to ever tell her that they are not attached. She had heard people declare in a grand, sweeping declaration:

'Of course I could walk out of here tomorrow and I wouldn't miss a thing'.

OF COURSE they would:

Their prized loo.

Because yes, it had to be admitted: Zzorroa was a bit homesick. She remembered her loo back home with its plastic seat and partly cracked broken ceramic top. She remembered the loo chain she pulled with a slight struggle at first, leading to a rushed release and onslaught, emitting the most grumbling sound before the sudden ease and eruption of a loud gush of water. She remembered. Perhaps she should have brought it with her.

A tear flowed down her face.

Dartagne was horrified. The poor girl must be desperately unhappy. Had she lost her way? He tried to speed up a little. Bigfortydeedee would sort her out.

Meanwhile he was wondering at the miracle that was Gargantua. How would he ever manage to understand how these giants could break all the rules of existence? That's why he preferred to stay in remote Singwolf. Gargantua was such a gift. How could it be that he was talking so young? How could it be that he could walk so young? So much for his valuable education.

His degree in medicine had included the very important

subjects of:

How to remove an ingrown toenail

How to prescribe antibiotics

How to tell people there was no remedy for a cold

How to tell people that they would have to wait ten years for an operation

How to tell people that they could only receive drugs of little use because they were affordable.

How to talk to patients after a pharmaceutical companies' drug lunch. (20 gin and tonics on the menu).

How to hire locums so doctors could carry on sleeping through the night.

How to become successful in business by buying surgeries with government funding and reselling them.

How to retire early on those profits and on grounds of sick leave.

How to put up signs warning patients of threatening behaviour enabling them to strike off any tricky customers who might need more than one visit a year.

How to boost their minimal salary of £1million per annum by taking on private clients two days a week and during their government-paid for holidays.

How to waste more government funds on filling in obligatory government forms for absolutely everything. This obviated the need for hospital beds and more tricky sick people.

How to delay sending results to sick patients for not being able to perform the operations necessary within government deadlines. This caused a bit of a Headline:

'Dead lying waiting for lifeline's deadline' or **'Confusing**

administrative matter of life or death'

How to retire without ever having got your hands dirty.

And so it was. Zzorroa in her world of loos and Dartagne in his world of medicine.

CHAPTER TEN

Of family, the lineage of Z, breathing in and breathing out, babygros with poppers and rainbow coloured pyjamas

With Gargantua's precociousness apparent, Pantagruel and Bigfortydeedee decided to have a serious discussion with Dartagne. Dartagne glided through the door at that very moment directing Zzorroa to the thingemeejiggy.

Freed from her lavatorial homesickness, she was introduced.

'I am Zzorroa with the extra Z' she explained.

'Ah, so you come from the lineage of Z,' Pantagruel exclaimed happily. I thought Eswhy Z was the last survivor but here you are. Might have known Z would have something up his sleeve. Have you seen the sword yet?'

Zzorroa opened her mouth in surprise, looking to Dartagne for succour.

He shrugged his shoulders as if to say they were always like that.

Gargantua announced his presence with a loud bang as he kicked the door open.

'Ah, my new friend, what a wonderful surprise to find you

here' he exclaimed as he rushed up and kissed a dazed Zzorroa's hand.

Pantagruel and Bigfortydeedee beamed with parental pride. He had exceeded all their expectations. Even his manners were exquisite.

This view was immediately shattered when Gargantua farted loudly refusing to go to bed. Ordinary parental disciplinarian authority was out of the question so they used a new foolproof alternative, beaming so many thoughts of love at him that he melted.

The hard stance that he presented deflated, similar to a fully pumped balloon crumpling to half size: that funny rubbery feeling if you were to touch it and poke your fingers in the layers. He visibly flopped and retired immediately.

Laying down on his bed to calm himself down, he tried to work out the silent force his parents had exerted on him.

He breathed in and out. He breathed in and out again. He tried it again.

What a miracle! He was able to breathe in and out. He hadn't noticed before how he breathed in and out. He tried it again and again. And again.

'I breathe in: fshfshfhs

I breathe out :

xhoooooooooooooooooooooooooooooooooooooooooooooop

'

'I breathe in: fshfshfhs

I breathe out :

xhoooooooooooooooooooooooooooooooooooooooooooooop

'

‘I breathe in: fshfshfhs

I breathe out :

xhooooooooooooooooooooooooooooooooooooooooooooooooop

’

‘I breathe in: fshfshfhs

I breathe out :

xhooooooooooooooooooooooooooooooooooooooooooooooooop

’

‘I breathe in: fshfshfhs

I breathe out :

xhooooooooooooooooooooooooooooooooooooooooooooooooop

’

‘I breathe in: fshfshfhs

I breathe out :

xhooooooooooooooooooooooooooooooooooooooooooooooooop

’

I AM ALIVE!

I BREATHE IN, I BREATHE OUT

EVERYONE IS ALIVE!

EVERYONE IS BREATHING IN AND BREATHING OUT!

I = THEM

WE ARE ALL EQUAL

DEMOCRACY RULES

Fshfshfhs

Xhooooooooooooooooooooop

As he concentrated on his breathing he remembered the world before labels. He found dignity and joy.

No matter that he had to go to bed early. No matter that he had to wear nappies and sailor suits. No matter that he had to wear babygros with poppers. No matter that the poppers always popped open and his nappy jutted out. And leaked. No matter that he had to wear blue. No matter that he had to wear stripes. No matter that he had to wear socks that were so short they kept on falling off. No matter that he sucked them and then dropped one to the ground and got a cold foot. No matter that he didn't have much hair and that the hair he had Bigfortydeedee insisted on tying up in a pony tail. No matter that he didn't wear a tie.

What did it matter what people thought? What did it matter what people wore?

We all breathed, we were all equal.

He jumped off the bed and ran through the 2546 clothes rails around his room. Clothes bought by parents and relatives for every eventuality. I can tell you of their vintage and labels because it was all recorded most carefully in the Cheltenham Gloscat Secret Offices.

Stellaris Mock Arty aged black stretch jeans
Dot Chez Grab Ana dry blue stretch jeans
Un Caro dry black stretch jeans
Man Solo Blabla Nic jodhpur hug jeans
Friendi 52 jeans
Leaveme bootcut jeans
Moche U Know nudie jeans
Die another Fun False Ten Birks skinny pins jeans
Cash Are ELLE hoochie bootcut jeans
Chacha Nil superfade lean jeans
Why Es El? vintage indigo lean jeans

Proud Aah vintage wash wide leg jeans
Lui Veut on? Super skinny jeans
Yoho Yaah Mi Motor zip jeans
Mar Xpensive albino wash jeans
Pinstripe pants
Turn up jeans
Trench coats
Military coats
Wool mix cigarette coat
Three quarter light jacket
Three quarter cropped jacket
Three hundred and sixty five polker dot pyjamas with large codpieces
Classic rim sunglasses
Black wrap sunglasses
Vintage shield sunglasses
Studded aviator sunglasses
Old tortoise sunglasses
Hai Tech trainers
Neink trainers
A deed Ass trainers
Poo my trainers
And one woolly hat which Bigfortydeedee had knitted.

But conversely, (a new word to appear out of his unconscious), what of all the prisoners who couldn't wear pyjamas? What of them? What was it like to have no change of clothes? What was it like not to have something to cover your dingleby dangleby?

It was decided. He found his paints and tipped rainbow

colours all over himself. From now on, until everyone in the world were free to wear what they wanted, he would wear his rainbow pyjamas with pride. He would wear his clothes with joy and dignity.

He jumped up and down with happiness and managed to leave elephant footprints on the parquet floor. Who knew if even tomorrow he would be walking on two or four feet?

Today he was a giant, tomorrow who knew?

Who knew anything?

He breathed in and he breathed out.

CHAPTER ELEVEN

OF GAMES

His bedroom was full of games of the day.

Monopoly

Scrabble

It

French skipping

A Football pitch which almost made the huge forest seem very small

A Netball set

Glove

Astrojax

Hoverdisc

Diabolo

Races

Jenga

Mousie Mousie

Magic tricks

Cluedo

Snatch

Yatse

Yo yo

Imaginary games

Croquet

Chess

Draughts

Snooker

Snakes and Ladders

La Marelle

Touche touche plus haut

Colin Maillard

Chaise Musicale

Bras de Fer

Doctors and Nurses

Dame

Mensch Argere Dich Nicht

Schach

Halma

Mastermind

Schwarzen Peter

Himmer und Holle

Korona

Les Osselets

Les Dominos

Colon de Catane (a partir de 7 ans)

Puissance 4

Trivial Pursuit Junior

Backgammon

Jeux de L'Oie

La courte paille

Cadavre exquis

Cartes Magiques

TicTacToe

Petit Bonhomme Pendu

War Hammer

OXO

Lotto

Bridge

Le Pouilleux ou le Valet puant or Black Jack

Le Rami Bridge

Canasta

La belotte

Le 21

Le 421

Le Poker

Le Poker menteur

Le strip poker (a partir de 5 ans)

Solitaire

Crocket

Badmington

Le diabolo

Le paquet de merde

Les petits chevaux

Jeu de L'oie

Le Loup

Bataille

Jeux des sept familles

Racing demon

Le huit américain

Whist

La crapotte

Le gin rummy

Chat Perché
Sardine
La Courte Paille
Murder
Chinese Whispers
Je vais au marché
Un deux trois j'ai vu
Gendarmes et voleurs
Cowboys and Indians (not pc though)
La main chaude
Getting warmer
C'est chaud c'est froid
Amstramgrampicetpicetcoligram
Cache tampon
Schatz Zucher
Jeu de piste
Course aux oeufs
Egg and spoon race (now forbidden for fear of viruses)
Le mouchoir
Le Jacquet
Le jeu de quilles
Billiards
Charade musicale
Le nain jaune
Yam
Pokemon
Lego
Playmobil
La ronde

Le cerceau
Sauter a la corde
L'élastique
Le Houla Hop
Cache cache
Pesapallo
Jouer aux billes pour avoir les cartaches
A table tennis table
A trampoline
A pedal car
A bouncy castle so large it could be seen from the Eiffel
Tower
A Swing
A kite
Arts and Crafts
A dressing up cupboard
Soft toys
A piano
Dominoes
Volleyball
A Flamenco guitar
An electric guitar
Toy soldiers
A rocking horse
Tiddlywinks

When Bigfortydeedee and Pantagruel came to wake him up in the morning, it took them an hour and fifty minutes to cover the terrain. As doting parents, it was all worth it because they did not want Gargantua to be without.

To be. To be without...To be or not to be...Tobeedoobeedoo. What is without? What is within? 'To be without' 'Out with?' 'Be out?'

Having waited so very long for a baby, they had unwittingly copied other parents who seemed to be caught up in the 'best of'.

And, dear reader, where did this idea of 'best of' come from? Was it that recent bestseller by Bugsy Ripoff entitled:

'A hundred easy ways to always have the best of'?

Do not think Pantagruel dim-witted, for his motivation was surely of the best. But if one looked at it more carefully, one might realize that the 'art of being' was as important as the 'art of being without' or the 'art of being with' and that the 'best of' presumed there must be a 'worst of' and what was the worst of? Being with or being without?

Pantagruel had chosen to follow the times and to copy his contemporaries but as he developed blisters visiting his son's bedroom he thought he might revise his opinion. What was 'best of'? Having a football pitch or not having a football pitch?

Some people saw it one way and others the other. Having a football pitch meant hiring people for the upkeep, laboriously painting the lines every year and getting council permission for the lighting. Not having a football pitch meant that his son might play in the free and natural forest all around them. He might make friends with the animals. But someone might abduct him or he might get some terrible rash.

Having the latest and 'best of' bouncy castle meant changing it every year to keep up with the Jones's. But that presumed that all the Jones's were the ones to keep up with. And what would be the opposite? Keep down the Jones's? Keep the Jones's?

God forbid! And if everyone had a bouncy castle would the world not be squeezed out of existence? Where to put them all? More arguments with the council because your blue bouncy castle covered a grain of land belonging to the Jones's green bouncy castle.

' Dear Sir,

It would seem that the neighbours have shown complete contempt for the boundaries of my land and are exceeding their boundaries by 100 blades of grass. Could you please see to this matter immediately? The situation is absolutely intolerable and we will take the matter to court.

Yours sincerely,

Mr. Down Jones wanting to be up Jones. Cross 'wanting' out: Down Jones up Jones's ...

Coffee table books: '*Views of the world from outer space*' would show nothing but different coloured bouncy castles dotted all over world cities. And multi-coloured deflated bouncy castles flying through space.

With telescopic microlenses, astex 48 extenders with Hasselbad digital cameras attached to the end, clever journalists could detect Mr Dow Jones x 1million / ¼ world population, pin between index and middle finger, deflating Mr Up Jones's castle. The coffee table books would cost enormous amounts to buy because to photograph the world through the fog of deflated bouncy castles required immense amounts of time and patience.

But really these two Jones's did not want to be up or down or between....

They just wanted to be king of the castle- forgive the inadvertent pun- king of their castle. They wanted moats and boundaries.

How we know our boundaries! That feeling when we walk into our home and our hair stands on end, our pimples stand up like geese. A hundred geese on our arms.

And we know someone is there... We pick up our sword and ask:

'Who's there? Qui va la? Quo vadis?'

Nobody answers, but we **know** they are there.

'Get out. This is my house, my space'.

If we could, we would put a tax on ghosts camping in. We would swat the air wildly screaming: 'Get out, get out, get out. I pay my council taxes you know. Don't think you can camp here for free. There's nothing free in this life, you know. Mark my words. Money is everything'.

So where did keeping up with the Jones's go? Evadis.

'What's mine is mine and what's yours is yours, so there'.

CHAPTER TWELVE

Of primary school, a genuine children's view on happiness

Pantagruel realized very quickly that Gargantua needed schooling and opted for the local village primary, thus avoiding the peripeteia of public schools. Gargantua would be with the Jones's. And the Smith's.

His future class had been given an important assignment- to write what made them happy or sad. This was included in the

SCHOOL MANIFESTO

TENKO ANNO DOMINI 19994

Please find within the authentically recorded conclusions of our dear pupils in a middle class Western school with no real problems where any parent could *safely* send their child for that purrfect education:

HAPPINESS IS

-when you smile and you're feeling good

-when my dog doesn't bark

-Christmas

-my cousin's house

-school

-when you get something special, like a dog or fish and you think you're going to care for it for a very long time

-when you feel 'this is really a good day'

-when you're not sad

-when you're lightheaded

-when you're healthy

-going on holiday

-riding my bike

-playing with people

-when people come to my house

-when I go to parties

-when my brother comes to stay

-when it's my mum's birthday

-when my dad takes me out

-when I have a marble

-when I don't go to school

-scoring goals

-football

-winning medals

-when I am sick on weekdays

-if I get a pet

-if I move house

-when I go horse riding

-going to see my grandad and nanny

-Harriet because she is sweet

-when Catherine comes round to play

-when I am on the computer

-when I'm at Brownies

-when my mum gives me treats
-when my friends come over
-when I go to the park
-when I go on holiday
-when I go country-dancing
-when I go past the river and see all the little ducklings in the river
-when I go swimming
-when I go to the beach
-when the sun is out
-when my room is tidy
-when I have lots of dinosaur toys
-when it's Christmas I like playing in the snow
-when I go on holiday to China
-when I cook
-pets
-when I have lots of fun
-when I eat ice cream
-toys
-my family
-when I give my mum a flying cuddle
-when I'm playing
-when my sister plays with me
-when I win a gold cap and medal
-when I can swim
-when I win a horse race
-when I get my rat out
-when I hold my baby
-if someone gives you chocolate

-if you play with your power ranger

-if you get a new motorbike for your power ranger

-if it was your birthday party

-when I see a rainbow

-when I see a cat

-when I do a good painting

-when I see a cat

-when I do a good painting

HAPPINESS IS ....IN THE WEST TODAY

JOIN OUR SCHOOL NOW FOR A HAPPY CHILDHOOD!

CHAPTER 13

OF UNHAPPINESS IN PRIMARY SCHOOL TERMS

Because the school wanted to be fair and show nothing but the truth, the opposite was included in the prospectus:

<u>**SADNESS IS**</u>

According to the free will of a certain state school's children aged six to eight

-when your face is frowning
-when someone's just taken one of your favourite toys
-when something really awful has happened
-when your favourite dog has gone away
-when my mum is mad at me
-when I have chicken pox
-when I get a shock
-when I do my work
-when I fall from a tree
-when you're eaten by a crocodile
-if a bear pushed you into a cave
-if your best toys get broken
-if your mummy went away
-when Oliver K. shouts at me
-when I fall over

-when I hear thunder

-when my brother died before I saw him

-mushrooms

-when I feel mad

-when I trap my finger in the door

-when I can't get to sleep

-when I fall in the mud

-when my mum goes away without me

-when I'm stuck in the traffic jam

-I don't like people

-going shopping

-when my sister pinches me

-when I get my name on the board

-getting changed after swimming

-when my brother's bossy

-when I get mosquito bites

-when I hurt myself

-when I hurt my knee and have to have stitches

-when I take my medicine

-when I go on stage

-when our rabbit was taken to another home

-when I have to eat sprouts

-when my dog barks

-my friends hitting me

-when there's stuffing on my plate

-the swimming pool

-gymnastics

-when mum makes the wrong breakfast

-when I go to hospital

-when someone's ill
-when my baby pulls my hair
-when it's raining
-when my rabbit died
-when I am sick
-when I hurt myself
-when I get bullied by my brother
-when my cat has to go to the vet
-when I am sick
-when we wait at the bus stop
-when Louis wrecks my bedroom
-when my dad goes to work
-when mummy goes to the doctor
-having a sister
-when I fall over
-when I'm stuck in a traffic jam
-when I take the wrong turning
-grown-ups
-getting bored
-people dying
-when I get told off
-when my dad is on holiday
-doing maths
-when your eye is poked out

'We like to believe our school is egalitarian. We believe in the community. The stronger must help the weaker and the elder the younger. Absolutely no bullying here' the headmaster boasted confidently as Bigfortydeedee had toured the school with Pantagruel.

'Oh darling, they *really* care, they have *principles*' she cried lakefuls.

It was agreed. Gargantua started on his third birthday. A twelve hour day.

Despite the deep desire to be like the others, Gargantua *was* a little bigger. One couldn't help but notice. A special needs teacher was appointed to his care and children were told very carefully not to mention the *fact-he-was-different* to him.

It only took two days for chaos to break out.

'You freak'

'You giant'

'You creep'

the other children taunted Gargantua on the playground.

Gargantua did not hesitate. He picked up the offending punks and spun them round on the end of his arm. Because of a shortage of staff (for cause of low wages, fear of being beaten up, inability to read or write, escaped through early retirement on disability pension, unsuitable ethnic minority, perverted sexual peccadilloes and so on) the children's behaviour went unnoticed.

But Gargantua had made it. He was *one of them*. They actually liked being thrown around on his arm. As says the mighty I Ching:

'Out of adversity comes good fortune'.

CHAPTER 14

OF SPECIAL NEEDS, INVISIBLES, 'IES,. FATE AND FETE AND KNICKERS

Gargantua could not remain invisible. Not only did he need a special needs teacher but he needed a special desk and classroom. This cost the school a lot of extra expense, particularly since he was clearly so bright and jumped up classes every few months. He seemed to know everything already or certainly was remarkably quick to learn.

Bigfortydeedee and Pantagruel approached the government for funding for his individual needs and discovered that for the essential building works to construct classrooms to fit him, there would be no problem but to aid his giftedness was impossible. No funds available.

The family made friends with everyone since they did not quite fit into either of the two types of parents. The two types became apparent when they joined the PTA.

There were the visibles who looked overweight, badly dressed, in need of a haircut, were round-shouldered from pushing buggies around and exhausted from too much unpaid work. They voluntarily presented a pallid insignificance.

And there were the invisibles: the *professionals*. Dada dada dada tata (theme tune to Batman in case you hadn't recognized it). They worked so hard they could never find time to pick up their children and on the rare occasion they did would look snootily in the air in front of them at nothing in particular.

For the invisibles it confirmed their lack of self worth whilst, IN FACT, it was because the professionals were.......

Choose from the following list and tick as appropriate:

a) so tired they could only keep their eyes open by looking upwards

b) so tied up in a secret love affair they were miles away

c) so insecure because they felt so guilty they were never around for their children and couldn't possibly look into the good mother's eyes

d) so high on achieving and being in control that they couldn't see what was in front of them

e) so drunk from the stressed life it was the only way not to fall over

f) so tied up with thoughts of work and the next deal that they were completely incapable of switching off

g) so anorexic from the tension of overwork, it was the only way to keep their trousers on and up

h) so depressed because they weren't successful **enough** to afford private schooling (despite the new jeep with clean tyres, new home, designer label clothes, working twenty hours a day and keeping all the younger and fresher up-and-coming upstarts wanting to replace them at bay)

The only thing that brought them together was the love of their Johnnies, Sammys, Louis's, Jacky's, Olly's, Dilly's, Annie's, Mary's, Markipoos, Scarletti's Tracey's, Timmy's, Bethie's and so forth.

And the 'ies insisted on parental attendance of the school fete. Fate? Nothing to do with fate. Fate does not exist. Nothing happens by accident. Everyone is here for a reason. Now do you not see why spelling should still be taught at school? It gets so complicated when such simple errors of understanding are made.

At the fête. Yes, fête with a hat on. Why a hat? Why a circumflex? Surely introspex was the order of the day. Circumflex, to flex around. Intros pex. Introductory music for the pectorals.

No the school band. And willing parents. Willing Willie to win. So they were quite willing to use their pectorals if Wee Willy Winning meant an early escape for secret Sunday siesta sex and sangria. No alcohol allowed at the fetes. More council rules.

So somehow the Visibles and Invisibles were roped into a tug of war.

'Come on mum, please'

'I'll tidy my room, mother, I promise'

'Dad, please show them how strong you are'

'Don't you think you should set the example, Daddy?'

'It's all for a good cause' —— the 'ies cried.

The team comprised

Beefy Danny	vs	Skinny Sanctus
Curly Madge	vs	Polly Perfect
Beergut Bob	vs	Swotty Otto
Barbie Doll	vs	Snooty Harriet
Silv the Stallion	vs	Damian Hearse
Angie Of Den	vs	Joanna Vit-Toyboy
Sugar Sweet	vs	Apple Whipper

And a few recalcitrant others who refused to give their name.

The headmaster blew the whistle.

As the players started to pull on the rope, the first man tottered and teetered.

'Come on dad' his kid yelled.

He drew himself up. For his son, anything. Anything? Yes anything.

The second man wavered and wandered.

'Go for it, daddy' his child cried.

He pulled himself straight. For his son, glory and honour. For his pride, all.

The second lady started to giggle.

'Keep at it, mum, don't let the side down' her Johnny cried, ensuring a good dose of maternal pride to give her extra strength.

The third lady's heel got stuck in the grass.

'Kick it off, mother and ignore it'

her yellow Blah Nic special flew across the ground.

But we forgot the rather vital fact that Gargantua had persuaded Pantagruel and Bigfortydeedee to join in at the last minute. Bigfortydeedee's huge cakes were so popular that they had sold in the first few minutes and people had given up on pelting Pantagruel as -the-one-one throws-sponges-at because they had run out of sponges (the school budget couldn't rise to it) and it was water off a duck's back.

Before any weather warning could be given, the strength of their enthusiastic pulling caused the opposite teams to be lassooed into the air like washing on a line, with their arms hanging on as the clothes pegs.

This surely would have been more than enough, if it hadn't been for the fact that all the children looking upwards could examine the state of the participants' underwear. And if more than enough weren't enough, the headmistress was one of those swinging the most high revealing, to all who cared to look, her suspiciously black g strings.

'Knickers, we can see knickers' the kids giggled.

And then, courtesy of Roald Dahl.....

She whipped her pistol from her knickers.

Pandemonium broke out. Police cars called. Headmistress handcuffed. Giants making a quiet disappearance.

CHAPTER 15

OF LOVE LYRICS, THE BLUES, BLUE AND ZIZIS

Pray you ask, what has happened to Dartagne and Zzorroa? Indeed, let us return to Singwolf a few years on. Not much had changed. Dartagne was obsessively running from place to place, working to save the world whilst Zzorroa was stuck, glued to the spot, in the Giants' guest room. Gargantua had taught her the art of breathing in and out and she found such repose in so doing that she remained stirred but not shaken for a few years, three months and three days. Bigfortydeedee brought her food and water and let her be, knowing that it was the moment for Zorroa to take time out and would do her far more good than her previous life and loo preoccupations.

There was just one problem. She had not killed off her obsession but transferred it. From loos to Dartagne. Sit as she might for month upon month upon year, her thoughts returned again and again to Dartagne. She had made the mistake of sending him a letter just before she began her training and had not received a reply.

Instead of finding solace in her breathing she developed an unhealthy repetitive addictive thought pattern.

Despite trying to *wash that man right out of her hair*, to *walk alone*, trying to be *alone again naturally,* declaring *I am not in love*, swearing *I will never fall in love again*, choosing to *walk on by*, to *move over darling*, insisting *you won't see me cry*, that she was *Stronger* and *Colourblind*, denying he was her *Hero*, that he was *All she had ever wanted;* she was still *Goin' Mad Blues*.

Blues it was. You might wonder why it was not Greens or Oranges but there were certain particular qualities to Blue or Blues. For one, it referred to a delightfully wistful era of music unsurpassed in history - given the name blues because of its close association with the French town, Nouvelles Orleans, where it was engendered and initiated.

Not many people know this but 'blues' actually then referred to the 'bleu' of decidedly unattractive bruises. The bleu were sometimes caused by too much blue absinthe and the resulting tumbles but more often, a blue mind, a bruised mind, usually referred to a bruised throat a la Holiday Billie. That is also why the Blues intelligentsia all smoked. If you look carefully in darkly lit jazz dens, you will notice the blue, not purple or white or red or any other colour but blue threads of smoke crawling through the air and expressing exactly the 'state of the blues'.

If you examine Muddy Waters wailing ' I'm a rooooooooad ruuuuuuuuuuuuuuuuunnnnnnnnnnner' you will see the blue smoke turn into the shape of a dragon. On the other hand if Holiday Billie were uttering: 'The bluuuuuuuuuuuues walked in and meeeeeeeeeeeeeeet me' you could literally observe smoke in the shape of blue ghosts being swallowed into her as she sang.

For the reason people died so atrociously from smoking and

secondary smoking was not the known reason of tobacco but the particular shade of blue smoke.

Secondly, it denoted the colour of the sky- with all its different hues. Light blue, dark blue, pale blue, RAF blue, grey-blue, peacock blue, electric blue, azure blue, bright blue, blue blue which was intended to clear the mind of its foggy haze, or smoke.

Thirdly, it referred to boys. Boys wore blue. Oh no! Zzorroa was back to thinking of Dartagne again. Why did boys wear blue? Particularly, why did boys still wear blue today? Even Gargantua's clothes had all been blue or blue and white. Not pink, for sure. The secret reason for this, which I shall now reveal, is that boys have members or plonkers or zizis or wibbeliwobbelies or dingleby-danglebies or things. Yes, well, we all know that. But what you don't know dear reader, unless you are a biologist, is that it has been proven irrevocably that when the boy or man accidentally leaves a minute droplet on his underpants and it leaks through to the blue of his clothes, the blue has a particular quality which leaves less mark. And since without the shadow of a doubt, not a single man has ever walked the earth who is not embarrassed by the 'leaking syndrome' in the days of no codpieces, the colour blue has remained steadfast as the primary choice for boys.

Dear me, I drift off the subject. I swear never to do this again but to write nothing but sequential and important relevant information for the reader. Yet, in a sense, this is just what was happening to poor Zzorroa: she wanted to concentrate on her breathing and could do nothing but be drawn back to her yearning for Dartagne.

She endlessly listed the causes women did not hear back from men. She tried to make it impersonal, to diminish the longing but it ate away at her, like a spiritual dildo.

ONE HUNDRED AND ONE REASONS FOR NOT HEARING FROM THE MAN YOU LOVE

1. He yawned and inadvertently swallowed her note
2. He thought her utterly boring
3. He didn't get her letter
4. He couldn't type
5. He was too embarrassed to ask his secretary to reply
6. Honour and valour had got the better of his existence and not a moment remained
7. He meant by silence not to hear from her again
8. He thought word unnecessary and used other means
9. He had lost his fingers
10. Dartagne had not told Zorrroa of his wild jealous dog
11. Dartagne had not told her of his wild jealous ex-girl-friends
12. He was teaching her to let go of expectations
13. RSVP was too old fashioned for words
14. He was teaching her to let go
15. He was in love with someone else
16. He had spilt glue over the keyboard and could no longer type a word
17. He had glued his fingers to the keyboard and could not move
18. He couldn't read

19. He couldn't write
20. He was dyslexic and didn't want to admit it
21. He was away travelling
22. He was too depressed
23. He was too jaded
24. He was too confused
25. He didn't like her red hair
26. He thought she wouldn't like his member
27. He thought she wouldn't like his bald patch
28. He had run out of pens that worked
29. He had run out of ink
30. He was seriously stuck on the loo
31. He was gay
32. He had no money
33. He had no property

(Since this particular subject is so very important it shall be continued in the next chapter)

CHAPTER SIXTEEN

OF MORE REASONS A MAN AVOIDS REPLYING TO A LADY or DARTAGNE TO ZZORROA

34. A dog had torn off his trousers and he didn't have another pair

35. His sword needed polishing

36. He couldn't be bothered

37. He preferred to watch the soaps

38. He preferred to day-dream

39. His mother wouldn't let him out of her sight

40. He had a twin who was really in love with Zzorroa already and he didn't want to cause acrimony

41. He had been selected for a trip to the moon

42. He had been struck with a poisoned arrow

43. He had been struck by the bells of Notre Dame and lay unconscious waiting to be rescued

44. He was blind

45. He didn't know what to say

46. He was involved in a secret mafia determined to keep ladies out

47. He was involved in 'the disillusioned man's brigade' which forbade contact with women

48. He had been secretly assassinated (oh no! too much to

bear) but, in her head, she was already attending his funeral and telling everyone he was the love of her life

49. In trying to rescue a fly about to fall prey to a spider web, he had stood on a chair and had fallen down and broken his leg. Despite medical intervention, he still could not walk more than a few metres

50. He still had the most severe case of Delhi Belly ever recorded

51. He was afraid of contracting the deadly flu virus and was walking around with a gas mask- but didn't want to admit it to anyone

52. He might be accused of rape when he had not even laid a finger on her

53. She had made the first move

54. He would only consider a virgin

55. She might have a pierced navel

56. She would stop him smoking

57. She would try and molly-coddle him. (what that had to do with a cod or Molly was beyond him!)

58. He had sent a reply via a flying pigeon but the pigeon was badly trained and delivered it to the wrong person- who subsequently also fell in love with him

59. He had a bad memory

60. He put it to one side to attend to later and forgot about it

61. He thought: 'I don't know (what to do) but I'll think of something' copying his great hero Indiana Jones

62. He believed the dictum: 'what you see is what you get' and he didn't see her

63. A week is a long time in politics

64. Her message contained the word ‘love’ and so was deleted as spam

65. His computer wiped all messages out

66. He could only reply in sign language (more of that later)

67. He had ordered a book on how to reply to women but the book was out of print

68. He wanted to appear cool and detached

69. He was stirred but not shaken

70. He didn’t know what he could offer her

71. A woman would take away from his passion for car washing every Saturday morning

72. He would have to think of presents to buy her

73. He just wanted to be ‘one of the lads’

73. Time, time time, no time

74. Mañana , mañana

75. Que será, será

76. He was neurotic lest she find a wet patch on him

77. He would have to clean up his house

78. She would make demands on him

79. He hadn’t got any aftershave

80. His razor was blunt

81. He had bad teeth

82. If he even replied to one letter, she would have him tied up like a dog on a leash.

83. Her breasts were not big enough

84. Her breasts were too big

85. She might have implants

86. He might need Viagra (it had been so long)

87. How could she ever be as good as his last love?

88. He only ever thought of his last love

89. Dreams were safer

90. He had piles

91. He wanted a twenty year old he could mould to his ways

92. He would think about it tomorrow

93. He had ants in his pants

94. He had bad breath

95. As a spy, he could trust no one

96. As a spy, he could take no one with him

97. He was on a journey to nowhere and women didn't like that

98. He was actually a robot and had no penis

99. The daleks, his owners, had warned 'exterminate' any female friend

100. And last but not least, he was a secret beast

101. This one does not really count but was added so there was no question of cheating over the correct number

The author would like the reader to realize that Zzorroa could have carried on this list for a very long time but decided to abridge at this point to save any beleaguered reader, if perchance they were suffering the same fate, from going completely mad.

Zzorroa sat in her corner waiting for her confusion to abate.
But alas, it seemed already to be too late.
(Iambic pentameter.)

CHAPTER SEVENTEEN

OF CLOUSEAU HOSPITAL, GARGANTUA'S PRIVATE TUTORS, KAMA SUTRA AND FLAGRANTE DELICTO

There was clearly no question of Gargantua returning to primary school. Not only had he outgrown it, but the headmistress had developed an allergy to anything giant and had been locked away in the Clouseau Hospital for Inspection. If ever anyone mentioned 'special needs' she reached for her knickers, which did not quite suit her professional position.

The two sets of parents had converged and were now 'The Universal PTA for Normality'. This meant they uniformly wore tight fitting jeans. Never ever again was a skirt to be spotted on the school playground.

The government found Gargantua a private tutor. Although it was considered old-fashioned, Gargantua learnt the 3 r's (reading, 'riting and 'rithmetic for the ignoramus among you). This was because recruitment difficulties had forced the employment of a 90 year old retired university physics lecturer by the name of Roughbottom. He had been a major in the war and believed in another out-of-fashion commodity: discipline. Gargantua had to stand up when he entered the room and address him as 'Sir'. 'Sir' was set in his ways. As he walked in and out of the classroom he would salute, punching his fist in the air and crying:

'ONWARDS AND UPWARDS'.

The first time he did this Gargantua wondered if he was meant to fly out of the classroom in hot pursuit. Apparently not, it was just a method of encouragement.

'Sir' also used to quote the classics:

'In my day,

when I was young,

at my school, Sgink, now that was a *real* school'

This would set him off chanting the psalm:

'Domine Jesu Christi, qui me create, redimisti, et preordinasti ad hoc quod sum. Tu scis quid me facere vis: fac de me secundum voluntatem tuam cum misericordia. Amen.'

Being a little aged meant that he often forgot what he was meant to be teaching and would ramble on again, about his youth.

'We used to really work at school in our day, not like you Gargantua. Beagling, cricket, tennis, rowing. I was Captain of the XI, hey what. Used to learn Ancient Greek then as well as Latin. How can you possibly know how the English language works if you don't know its roots? You're the first generation not to study the classics and know your history. It will be your undoing. As Healee said, if you don't know your history, you can't run a country. Greengrocery is not sufficient.

ATTENTION!

HOP TWO THREE FOUR. THAT'S IT. GET THE BLOOD GOING. PEOPLE TODAY DON'T EXERCISE ENOUGH. TOO MUCH SEDENTARY ACTIVITY. HANDS IN THE AIR! HANDS DOWN! LEGS UP! (WHOOPS, I'LL GET SACKED FOR THAT ONE) LEGS DOWN! NOW

RECITE: AMO, AMAS, AMAT, AMAMUS, AMATIS, AMANT. WHOOPS, I'LL GET SACKED FOR THAT. DELETE, GARGANTUA, NOT PART OF THE CURRICULUM TODAY. RECITE THE ALPHABET IMMEDIATELY. HOP TO IT! 2+2=4, 4+4=8, 8+8=16. REMEMBER THAT! OH, THAT TAKES ME BACK TO THE AURORA BOREALIS OF 1910. REMEMBER THAT, BOY? NO OF COURSE YOU WOULDN'T. YOU'RE ALL USELESS TODAY. WHAT YOU NEED, GARGANTUA, IS A WAR. THAT WOULD TOUGHEN YOU UP.'

At that moment he whipped a stick from his wooden desk and tried to pull down Gargantua's trousers.

'YOU'RE NOT LISTENING, YOU'RE NOT LISTENING, GARGANTUA. DON'T LOOK SO INSOLENT, BOY. DISCIPLINE, IT'S ALL DISCIPLINE.'

Roughbottom had met his match. He was out for the count before he could count and quickly replaced.

Supply teacher Seamus Sloppy was about thirty, had long hair, wore jeans and a striped T shirt. His teeth were yellow from smoking too many roll-ups and his fingernails cracked and black from doing DIY at home. Property prices being so high, he had been forced to build his own hut in a friend's back garden and lived there with his missus and five brats.

He never really wanted to be a teacher but had drifted into it because the teacher training grants were so tempting. Boy, that year had been hard. But since then, it kind of worked out. He managed to eke his living with the odd supply teaching here and there. No need to prepare too much for the lessons and the ability to moan about the system as much as possible. This particular number was very attractive. Highly unlikely Gargantua would start throwing a wobbly and bring out a knife. His hands shook. Yeah, he'd rather stay alive and that meant ignoring the bullying whilst interfering as little as possible.

'Watcha, pal, he thumped Gargantua on the back. How' ye doing?'

'Very well, Sir' Gargantua replied.

'Cool it, Gargantua, no need to be so formal, call me Shame, okay?'

'Yes, Sir, I mean, Shame.'

'I've brought some books along for you to study, but maybe best if you keep it between you and me? Know what I mean?'

Out of his back pocket he produced the latest 'Kama Sutra', 'One hundred types of Belgian beer', and a back copy of the now defunct: 'Socialist Worker'.

In the following week he brought along videos of live examples of graduate love-making and took Gargantua on a field trip to visit Marx's tomb. As course work, it was absolutely necessary for Shame and Gargantua to pass by the Kriek and take a steamer on the Gueuze, sampling the various beers, getting piste in the Trap which inevitably resulted in Shame's unexpected 'Mort Subite'.

Still, the government pension would look after his children.

Next, the government provided a lady tutor.

Laura LaSainte was immaculately turned out with lipstick to match her perfectly ironed outfits. Her cheeks were a healthy rose, her clothes fadingly flowery and summery, reminding one of times gone by: golden, happy, carefree Ashley days. Around her neck she wore a perfectly polished silver cross and her smile was natural and perpetually on offer.

She was born to teach
And loved teaching
And loved children
And loved her classroom
And loved setting homework
And loved the artwork she hung on the walls
And loved the flower arrangements fresh from the forest
And loved the alphabet written in perfect cursive script
And loved each and every child she taught who would do
ANYTHING to have her smile beamed down upon
them
And was loved by every parent who knew their children
were in safe hands
And was loved by every male who couldn't help but feel
protective towards her
And was loved by every female who wished they could be
more like her.

Laura LaSainte was a *good* person. She exemplified the government's belief that teaching was possible. The government even employed actresses to mimic her on promotional party broadcasts.

Pantagruel and Bigfortydeedee relaxed at last. Nothing could go wrong with LaSainte, eager for a 'nice little job' after maternity leave. They left the two together.

But Gargantua, fresh from kama sutra studies, found her comfortables too delectable and she found his member giantly enthralling and totally irresistible. Unbeknownst to anyone but her victims, LaSainte had always had a penchant for schoolboys and a previous scandal with somebody under-age had had to be hushed up. Because of her public profile, it was kept out of the papers.

LaSainte became la Sinner.

Gargantua completed a healthy part of his education, if not curricular activity.

He would never forget that idyllic summer, disturbed only by Bigfortydeedee finally wondering at the silence and finding them in flagrante delicto. And so LaSainte, too, was evicto.

CHAPTER EIGHTEEN

OF PANTAGRUEL'S BET, COFFEE, JCLOTHS, SUGAR AND DONKEYS

The government had given up
on a 'size impaired' or
'mentally large' or
'size disadvantaged'or
'special sized support'
because they were too short of funds, there was too little demand and they were helpless before such a giant obstacle (whoops, we mustn't mention that word *giant* for fear of reprisal from all politically correct departments). Or it could have been that Gargantua had learnt the important art of hacking and had fiddled the forms so they wouldn't notice he was no longer receiving formal teaching.

He was so advanced anyway that he decided to complete his education watching the television.

Satellite allowed him to pick up fifty languages in three years and world history in twelve months. He learnt cooking (vegetarian, vegan, Italian, Indian, Pakistani, Bangladeshi, Thai, French, Chinese, Japanese, Vietnamese, indeed all types but English because it didn't appear to exist). He learnt advanced modern art and was even entered for the 'Turnitover Prize' from children's programmes on 'how to cut up paper' and 'how to draw in five easy steps' and 'how to throw paint on paper'.

Using his century-old renown for farting gases, he conducted healthy science experiments and he became a world expert in biology by watching hospital soaps and crime thrillers specializing in dissecting dead bodies. He learnt manners from his parents but refused to use them, leaving them utterly disconcerted.

So disconcerted in fact that Pantagruel returned to the pub. Over a few pints of beer with his male cronies, he admitted:

'I can't stand the way of the world today. It seems to me that all the children's learning is mere stupidity and their wisdom like an empty glove.'

De Vere, a fellow pub frequenter and local farmer, suggested that he send over his son, Miles to see if indeed Pantagruel need be so desolate.

'Let them have a debate and see who knows what. Let us see if Gargantua is such a fool or if indeed Miles knows a lot more. For often a few years' education can be completely wasted. Let's see the difference between your old-time nonsensological babblers and the young people of today'.

Pantagruel liked the idea and invited Miles over the following day...

'How do you do, Sir' Miles volunteered, proffering a hand as he entered.

'Very well, very well. Now come on, let's get to the point quickly. Let me introduce you to my son and let's have this contest.'

Miles was immaculately turned out in a spotless white shirt, a polkerdot tie and navy merino wool trousers with a perfect pleat at the front. He even wore a double- breasted navy blazer with gold buttons. His hair was cut short, with a fringe straight back and sides.

'Gargantua, it is the wish of our fathers that we spend some time together. How pleasant for me to have such an opportunity. I must first praise you for your fine clothes, of such resplendent rainbow colours. And what about your fine face, scrubbed clean with Brut soap and smelling no less than divine. As for your hair tied neatly in its pony tail, it shines more than if you had used Brylcreem.'

Gargantua ignored him completely, sniffing noisily and to avoid blowing his nose, wiping his arm horizontally from elbow to the tip of his index finger across the tip of his nostrils. As he lay his arm down, a wet patch was visible running along the aforementioned line. Still, he sniffed again.

Bigfortydeedee brought them some coffee, urging them to sit down.

Miles sat, back perfectly straight, at table and reached for the napkin in front of him, unfolding it neatly across his knees. Gargantua hunched his shoulders with both elbows at flat right angles on the table in front of him.

Miles offered the jug of milk to Gargantua before serving himself. Gargantua just grunted, slopping what- seemed- like- a -pint into his mug whilst spilling a copious amount over the wooden surface. He then left the jug in front of him for endless minutes until he remembered and slid the jug across the table to Miles who carefully poured his whilst ensuring the mug was securely on a drinks mat.

Bigfortydeedee made secret signs to Gargantua who went to the kitchen and picked up a wet, unwrung jcloth on the sideboard and swayed it over and around the spill in a large figure of eight. Picking the now-over-soaked-milky-watery jcloth up, he flung it across the room into the kitchen where it landed in a heap on the floor. The mark on the table looked worse and larger and even more as if the imprint would become indelible.

Bigfortydeedee's blood pressure rose.

'Would you like some cake?' she offered, cutting up a huge chocolate cake with a silver knife.

'Why, thank you, Mrs.Bigfortydeedee, that would be most agreeable' Miles replied, leaning over to take the plate from Bigfortydeedee's hand.

'What was that, Gargantua? I didn't quite hear your reply' she asked.

Gargantua grunted.

As Miles took the small fork by his plate and turned it diagonally, enabling him to cut into the fudgy crumbly substance, Gargantua grabbed the next slice from his mother's knife and stuffed the whole lot in his mouth.

As he chewed, bits of brown substance slipped over the edges of his lips and down his front, forcing him to wipe his mouth on his hands and his hands on his clothes whilst bits of cake fell to the ground. He then stood up and trod on them. His napkin remaining untouched next to his plate.

Walking to the CD player he put on 'God save the Queen' by the Sex Pistols at full volume and sat down again.

'Delicious cake' Miles spoke loudly.

'Thank you, Miles, how kind' Bigfortydeedee yelled across the cacophony of sound.

He wiped his mouth carefully on the napkin.

Gargantua grabbed the bowl of sugar and using the spoon in the sugar bowl, as opposed to his own, spilled three large spoonfuls into his mug and stirred noisily and lengthily. He then replaced the wet spoon in the bowl.

'Could you pass me the sugar?' Bigfortydeedee demanded, upset she had to ask at all.

Gargantua took the bowl between his thumb and middle finger and spun it along as if trying to shoot in a bowling alley. Golden specks of organic Demerara sugar splattered across the table as the bowl landed, half-tipped up, in front of Bigfortydeedee's mug. She reached for the spoon and found hardened grains stuck to the silver so that her spoonful became a mountainful. So many grains in fact that as she filled the spoon up and dropped it into her mug, she wondered angrily if she had the right amount or had taken too much. Half the mountain remained stuck to the spoon whilst a few specks fell into the desired receptacle. She tasted it. No, she had to start again.

Why couldn't her Gargantua be more like Miles?

Her blood pressure rose some more.

'So, Gargantua, do tell me what you have learnt through your home education?

Have you completed the international Bac or the minimum A'level requirements? Nothing would give me more pleasure than going through the set texts with you and comparing our knowledge.

Do you play chess? I have just won the 'Brainbox of the year' award permitting me to gain a scholarship to the best university. Such a splendid opportunity.' Miles soliloquised.

This speech was delivered so clearly and precisely, with such perfect erudition and grammar, with such totally exemplary elocution, in sublime traditional Queen's English that he seemed more like a child of Victorian, Renaissance or Edwardian time than an ordinary schoolboy of today.

Gargantua licked his fingers noisily whilst stretching across the table and cutting himself another slice of cake.

At last he looked at Miles's face and was so overcome by his earnest stance and successfully starched laundered shirt that he could not contain himself and burst into uncontrollable paroxysms of laughter.

The force of his laughter mixed with the two slices of chocolate cake caused him to release a strong juicy fart. He pulled the back-to-front baseball cap down over his face and it was no more possible to draw a word out of him than another fart, albeit on this occasion from a dead donkey.

And so the conclusion was this. Pantagruel was forced to compliment De Vere on his perfect son and concede defeat. He also decided to take Gargantua's education into his own hands by taking him on a journey to L'Undone.

CHAPTER NINETEEN

OF TRAVEL, MERCI DES, FARTS IN BY- WAY- OF- A- LAUGH, MARE BRITANNICUM

For the next few days all that could be heard was the sound of worn quotations, songs and book titles from the normally tranquil Pantagruel. Emanations such as:

It's all in the travelling, not in the getting there.

Journey without goal.

Travel broadens the mind.

Somewhere over the rainbow.

The road less travelled.

It's a hard rain that's gonna fall.

Gulliver's Travels.

Gullible's travels.

The travels of my aunt.

To travel but not to arrive.

Edelweiss.

GI Blues

The girl from Ipanema

Barefoot in the Park

Three coins in a fountain

The rain on the plane

Madison Blues

Pirates of Penzance
While shepherds washed their socks by night
Bye Bye Blackbird
Pennsylvania 6-5000
Carolina in the morning
Fiddler on the roof
Don Quixote
Wandering star
He played his ukulele as the ship went down
In the shade of the old apple tree
It's a long way to Tiperary
Bridge over Troubled Water
Chimchimcheree
Tuxedo Junction
Chicago
Ticket to Ride
La Paloma
Guantanamera
Jailhouse Blues
Au revoir Paree
The Hills are alight
A foggy day in London town
Au clair de la lune
Avalon
Zipedidooda
You will never walk alone
Jerusalem
Edelweiss
White Christmas

Underneath the arches
Chattanooga Choo Choo

And more. But lest the author should bore the reader, the story shall continue.

Pantagruel had had the foresight to approach a car company who had been Merci Des producing a custom-made vehicle. They even offered it gratis wanting all publicity possible when the giants decided to venture outside their secret residence.

The car was of shining silver, as large as six elephants and as tall as two giraffes, with fifty extra-strong wheels on rubber rollers like those on a tank. These were coated with circular skis to give extra gliding power. The windows were made of rainbow coloured glass allowing invisibility to external onlookers but perfect visibility from the inside.

The gear stick was made out of fake Dalmatian tail and the interior of rainbow brush-cotton (to match Gargantua's clothes and so offer him extra protection). It was also remarkably comfortable for the derriere and avoided that painful plopping sound when women removed their glorious buttocks from the clasping ribbed plastic seats.

The 'special feature' was the sound of the engine. Contrary to expectations, it was not a loud roar but rather the tranquil purr of a cat.

If this description astounds you, you would be even more surprised by the making of the gear stick which took at least five hundred men forty days to assemble. It had 101 spots, placed at precise points to enable Gargantua to change gear with distinct ease.

The car was ceremoniously called 'Stinkbomb' for the bomb Merci Des would make whilst the giants created a stink. For this, Pantagruel was truly thankful.

Pantagruel had insisted Bigfortydeedee accompany him as well as Dartagne and Zzorroa. It was, after all, their native land. All three were full of trepidation for differing reasons.

Reckoning the car didn't even need a test drive, they drove straight up the Sun motorway, crossing large tracts of land and taking a break at Verse I to eat some cake in a large and gloriously ornate room full of mirrors and gold. This was the perfect motorway stop-off for checking their attire before reaching their ancestor's old stomping ground of Paris.

The Perilouspheric brought them straight to the centre where they stretched their legs by the Seine and By Way of a Laugh, accidentally leant against the bells of Notre Dame, causing them to ring at an unusual hour. The caretaker, who happened to be rather hunchbacked, panicked, remembering a notoriously famous occasion when the untimely peel had been no accidental knock. (Some of you may need to refer to Penguin Classics to read the story chapter 18). An old and sore Bonne came rushing to his rescue but there was no need.

Gargantua and co had sped forth with spirit to Dunkirk after dining on treifle up a famous tower.

As they contoured the Perilouspheric once again, they pressed the anti-polluter button set up by Queue as an extra secret weapon. The entire smog in Paris was instantaneously absorbed through their back pipe, transpollinated and ejected as a large gaseous eruption causing the speed to double from 40kmp to 400 kmp. As those technicians among you will know, this rebroke the barrier of sound, discovered by the E=MC2 photon of 1 Stone to the power of noble 1921 permeating through the interface of causality factor solaris 15 for Amber tanned specialists, and created no more disturbance than a disagreeable smell lasting less than a second.

No less wondrous was the car's ability to develop eleven flipper fins and so turn into a fast pelting boat across the ocean. They bumped into old family friends by the name of Asterix and Obelix, Gaulish warriors and an infamous pirate vessel, a Phoenician vaissele (which Gargantua refused to do) and a galere romaine.

Hearing cries of 'A L'Abordage' they speeded up, narrowly avoiding the Admiral's fleet 200 years on. Pif paf, blam, bong, gloup, gloup, gloup (French version), Bom bom, bong, flop, flop, flop, craaaash, tagadong, tobodoubodou, tchac tchac, thoc, thoc (English version), Land ahoy! Men overboard! Giddy goat's horns! Nous sommes fichus! The 'mare britannicum' left them all with that sinking feeling.

It was in such a peaceful manner that they erupted over the Dover Cliffs.

CHAPTER TWENTY

OF L'UNDONE, PARKING METERS AND UNIVERSITY COURSES

Reaching Dover Cliffs, they flew through customs and sped along the A2. Avoiding a plague of drunken joy riders and koan after cone, they took another break at Greenwich deciding they had made mean time.

It took a little longer to navigate the circular to reach L'undone Town, glorious and grand multicultural metropolis of the modern modus vivendi. Winner of many prestigious awards for random events and sites such as Olympic City, royal weddings and divorces, Horrids, the blitz, the tube, Buckandrun Palace, the Bloody Tower, Parlelimpcement, Cornyby street, the Doome, Madame Tussle's waxworks, Queue, the Serpent, Ken'sintown, Bricked Lane, So Hoh, the Taight, Shake and Spear's Gob , the Risktz, Fortnoman and MySon and even more royal weddings and divorces.

Being efficient and organized, Dartagne had bought lots of coins to ensure secure parking at the metering points.

Pantagruel read from a list of various university courses starting in the autumn. It would just be a question of checking out the colleges. They decided to drive straight to SPLASH, new university specializing in useful modern subjects, vital ingredients for employment in this day and age. The prospectus read:

LIST OF BA'S AVAILABLE

How to boil eggs
How to make a golf course
How to paint a wall
How to change a nappy
How to turn on your computer
How to make a baby
How to fill in forms
How to make a shopping list
How to load aeroplane meals onto an aeroplane
How to speak the Queen's English
How to spell
How to massage figures.
How your postcode can damage your child's future.
Terminological inexactitude.
Excessorexia or the desire to be perfect.
How an allergy free cat is not to be sneezed at.

'We are proud of our new red brick university status and believe in upholding the latest government policies. We believe in dropping standards and upping bureaucratisation. We vehemently deny Kingsley Amis's quote: 'more means worse'. Our university needs YOU. Our quotas need you. We need numbers to keep our buildings afloat. Your money goes on our infrastructure. Don't worry if you have no academic skills and are of the lowest common denominator, we will still

take you on. You will still learn basic skills and pass your degree with honours. The bottom line is always money. We will teach you how to make money. Money makes the world go around so please keep our coffers filled and learn by our example. '

Waltzing through the entrance, they asked the receptionist to let the chancellor know they had arrived and were delighted to find that the library was completely full: students pouring over their work today as if there were no tomorrow. Even the chairs in the reception were occupied. And come to think of it, couples were sitting on benches outside in the opposite manner to the one one would expect- in other words- back to front- and they were kissing.

'Oh, they don't have enough living accommodation at home so they use our benches'

'A good sign' thought Pantagruel.

They waited. And waited. And waited. Mr. PeterPanPrinciple did not turn up.

'Could you *please* call Mr. PeterPanPrinciple again?' they asked the grouchy, bashful, sleepy, dopey and grumpy receptionist.

With a loud huff, she spoke into a tannoy.

'Could Mr. PeterPanPrinciple come to reception please, where Mr. Pantagruel, Mrs.Bigfortydeedee, Gargantua, Zzorroa and Dartagne are waiting to see him?'

A boy of around twenty passed them by with big shiny blue eyes, blonde spiky hair and square navy blue suit and tie.

'Ah, you must be new students?' he asked.

‘Potential new student’ Gargantua replied.

‘Great.Take one thousand of my leaflets. Spread the word. I belong to a great organization that could transform your vision. NFL. NERDS FOR LIFE. We’re the virus club. We need to update the hyperdrive so we can infiltrate the vortex of the main frame hub of the NFL foundation. It’s really taking off, very popular, supremely hectic. It’s really hectic blood. That’s hectic from the west side crew, straight down to the east side, blinging massive.We’ve got a great teacher. He’s wicked, hot diggedy dog diggedy. I recommend it. We’ll give you 30 megabites of ram and a laminated personal identification card - a beautiful nerd label. Pretty tidy girls too. So I’ll see you at the next meeting’ he smiled jovially.

Gargantua smiled back.

Pantagruel smelt a rat.

Gargantua examined the glossy leaflet:

NERDS FOR LIFE

‘You can be happy now. Forget your worries and learn to be calm. Come to our teachings Thursdays at five. You won’t regret it. It’s hectic. LET’S EXPLORE HOT DIGGEDY HOT DIGGEDY’.

A photo showed many glossy smiling faces and bright white teeth. All blonde haired and blue eyed.

He handed it to Dartagne. Dartagne coughed immediately and handed it straight over to Pantagruel.

‘Thought so. My word, they’re clever. Doesn’t it all look so attractive: ‘Nerds for Life’

My Foot.

Mon oeuil.

Mein Boobi.

Mi cabeza.

Moy Pushkinski. What is wrong with everyone's life to need a New Nerd Life? What is a New Life? What is a nerd? What are they founding?'

Bigfortydeedee made a grab for the leaflets because she couldn't bear to be kept out of it. She immediately burst into repeated and uncontrollable sneezes.

Such was the force of her third 'atishoooooooooo' that each and every library boffin was huffed, puffed and blown against the walls.

CHAPTER TWENTY ONE

OF CHANCELLORS, FAKE, RESEARCH AND PARKING

As the assembled students were sprayed back into their chairs, ankle deep in a pool of Bigfortydeedee's sneeze, Pantagruel addressed them:

'I am so sorry that my wife's sneeze has caused you such discomfiture. She was overcome by the effect of a shiny leaflet'.

The students all turned away disgruntled, shaking their feet dry and pointing their shoes at the radiators whilst the water tumbled out of the door into the reception area, developing a flatter and thinner consistency, similar to a runny egg yolk. A lone cleaner appeared and mopped the moisture dry.

Meanwhile a particular gentleman of a certain age and disposition (between forty and sixty to be precise) and certain standing (he was upright but a fraction bent to be precise) with a certain number of strands of hair (about 35 to be precise) and a certain protuberance around the stomach area (about 30 centimetres over the trouser line or maybe 40 to be precise) and a certain amount of shoddy shaggy and shaky toggle buttons on his suit jacket (six with two missing to be precise) tottered forward with a certain self-assurance (not for life):

'I am Mr. PeterPanPrinciple. You have rather dampened our

mood this morning. We were quite happy bobbing along....Hehem.

Sorry to keep you waiting but I had to complete my quota for the year end or my job would be in jeopardy. I'm writing about research into research. There is so much research going on, it's hard to find time to keep up with the research about research.

The alternative, of course, would be to do nothing, just sit in a chair as a chairperson, a profession with even less standing, so I persist in trying to keep up with the research.'

'And what is the research about?' Pantagruel enquired.

'Oh, that doesn't matter. Long gone are the days when people did research and wrote books because they had something to say.'

'So you can't tell me your speciality?'

'Well, yes, keeping up the quotas and keeping a roof over our heads. That's the second reason I was late. I was fixing the computer numbers in the library. The students are an experiment. How many students can fit in to as small a zone as possible before spilling into the reception area? Good exercise for them too. Might get into the Guinness Book of Records to beat the 56 people who got into a mini.'

And the third reason is that I was scared, scared lest you be the 'powers that be' about to abolish my department. You see, they've abolished the Law department, the Biology Department, the Physics department, the Maths department and the Chemistry department because they were doing so badly- their quotas weren't sufficient.

Of course there's an argument for supporting those doing

badly but that doesn't apply today. So now virtually all that is left is the administrative department. And all the new useless subjects everyone wants to take because they can't study anything meaningful.'

He tried to take breath and drops of saliva dribbled down his face.

'We need to RATIONALIZE and ABOLISH SUBJECTS' he spat out, allowing spittle to cover Bigfortydeedee's hands.

She surreptitiously wiped them on her clothes. After all, she could hardly complain.

'And we were wondering about these leaflets? The NERDS FOR LIFE?' Pantagruel asked.

'Yes of course, very popular, so popular, very wealthy, offer us gifts all the time. Good group growing all the time. Nice bottle of Scotch they gave me. I think the term the youth use today is 'they're sick'. Apparently that means they're amazingly good.'

More dribble fell onto Bigfortydeedee's hand.

'So, Gargantua, what course are you interested in?' Mr PeterPanPrinciple finally enquired.

Dartagne thought this a good moment to slip away and fill up the parking meter. Reaching the spot, he found an inspector writing out a ticket.

'Hello there, what are you doing? Aren't I on time?' he asked.

'If you just look at your watch, gov, you'll see you're not. Four minutes late. Four minutes late. Count yourself lucky, gov, if you pay within 14 days it's only £500. And if you don't move your car now, you'll be done again. Look: Feeding the meter prohibited'...

'But my watch says we have four minutes to go.'

'Well, Sir, don't mind me, but it's too late. I've written the ticket now and you're done for. Got a mobile? You could always check with that sexy lady who drips delectable delight with the drooling drone of her tone.

'At the third stroke, the time sponsored by accurist will be dot dot dot...'

Meant to be very accurate, they say, but then you weren't here when I started writing out this ticket, were you Sir? You've had your chips, if you'll pardon my French. Your pay cheque is frite or chipped. Forget about the fish. Even if you should want a banger, you've lost one- for a bit, that is. Mind you there is a very good take-away up the road if you prefer. Kebabs.'

Dartagne, still far too gallant to lose his temper returned to the inside fray. And the last time he had checked the time on the telephone it had been a man's voice.

Mr. PeterPanPrinciple was getting a little hot under the collar. The remaining buttons on his jacket were bursting at the seams.

'Well, I'm sorry, Gargantua, if we don't do languages anymore but studying languages definitely became archaic and invalid in about 20001. Everyone speaks English nowadays, don't you know. Everyone. And if they don't, that's tough. We're global now. That means everyone speaks our language. Definitely. That's definite.

'But what about China, India and Brazil to name but three?'

'They're sending all their students to us. Haven't you

noticed our foreign quota? They're our bread and butter. And since the war, to eat bread without butter wouldn't do. Jam is pretty much a prerequisite now too. And we couldn't live without dough, could we? So give me your dough as well and stop wasting time barking up the wrong tree. Sorry, I know you don't speak dog language and there are no trees left around us, but I'm sure you get the gist'.

Dartagne whispered to Pantagruel who slipped out immediately. He moved the car a few spaces away and placed more £2 coins in the machine. They walked back in.

By now the students had assembled behind the Chancellor and seemed to be standing in line. And as they stood in line they began to look remarkably like monkeys. Monkeys and more monkeys. And each and everyone was carrying an egg.

CHAPTER TWENTY TWO

OF MONKEYS, GERMS, TOWING AND KAMEDEN

The monkeys seemed to be advancing towards them, jogging their arms in unison, an egg clutched in their left hand and producing spittle.

The giants were being threatened. Zzorroa stood behind Gargantua and next to Dartagne who remained calm and alert, Mr. Cuddles jutting out of his right hand pocket.

'Are you menacing us?' Pantagruel enquired.

'No, no, no, of course not. Just encouraging you to join up. Woudn't want you to miss out on the twenty percent discount if you join today. Why don't you sign here now, Gargantua?'

'Because I don't want to.'

'Of course, of course, there's no hurry, but just sign this form now and it will all be all right. Thirty percent off. And we're going to see our elephant today. He's at home but we're looking for his footprints in the forest.'

'For goodness sake, we live in a free society, a democracy. You're not my cup of tea' Gargantua spoke up.

'Exactly- that's why you can choose to join us. We're your cup of coffee.'

'I don't want to hear about cups of tea or coffee, but about true learning. What is my son to learn here that could possibly be of value to him?' Pantagruel enquired ardently.

Each monkey replied in turn:

'ABC'

'DEF'

GHI

JKL

MNO

PQR

STU

VWX

And Y and Zee

Chanted in Sesame Street American tone.

'WE ARE HAPPY IF YOU PLEAEASE. SIAMESE'

'WE ARE HAPPY IF YOU PLEASE SIAMESE'

'WE ARE HAPPY IF YOU PLEASE SIAMESE'

'BALA, BALA, BALA, BALA, BALA.
BALA, BALA, BALA, BALA, BALA.'

Thoughts and sensations. Conflicting and increasingly conflicting thoughts and sensations.

'Stay calm and undistracted. They are all giving too much credit to their thoughts' Pantagruel yelled.

With dialogue impossible, the family backed off and out, scooping up Dartagne and Zzorroa and making a beeline for the exit. ZZZZZZZZOOOOOOOOOOOOOOOOOOOOOMMMMMMMM-MMMMM.

Meanwhile only an empty space greeted the spot where Pantagruel had parked Stinkbomb.

Stinkbomb was being towed away on a tank.

'Hey, what are you doing?' Gargantua asked the employees in bright jackets with luminous £ signs on their chests.

'Can't ya see, man: wee're towing away your car.'

'But why?'

'Because ya're four seconds ovaa da hour, man'.

'But you can't tow it away!' Gargantua exclaimed.

'Oh but we can and we are.'

'But we need to get away' Gargantua explained.

'Datsa what dei all say, man'.

'So what to do now?' Dartagne enquired politely.

'Here's da card, man. Just get along to the pound as quickly as possible and collect it dere.' The attendant encouraged.

'The £. The £?' Pantagruel asked.

'It's okay, we can be there in a jiffy' Dartagne consoled.

Preempting his words, Zzorroa had dived into the Post Office Tower, bought two jiffy bags and handed one to Dartagne.

'Two steps to the left, five to the right, two more straight on with us gliding on the jiffy bags and we'll be there.' She told them.

Dartagne beamed at her. She swooned.

They reached the £ before the tank did. It was hidden up a shady alley with badly tarmacked road surfaces, lots of muddy puddles and grim cement prefabricated buildings. The £ sign shone clearly and luminously on the front entrance as it did on all the employees' jackets. They walked in.

More £ signs shone everywhere.

'I think I'm getting a head-ache' Bigfortydeedee cried.

'Just sit here, darling' Pantagruel offered as he waited his cue in the queue.

'We are in Britain after all' he adjusted.

People ahead of them handed over credit cards and at the magic words:

'You can go-o-o and collect your kaa now, ma-am'

cried in ecstasy, angel delight and whipped cream, as if they had found their long lost child.

It was Pantagruel's turn.

'We've been told to collect our car from here' he told the £ employee behind the counter.

'Dat will bee £1 000.'

'But how can that possibly be?' Pantagruel asked.

' Dat's eeeeasy, Sir. You were in a location of contravention. Your paid for time had expired. On top of that, we had to employ a tank to move such a large vehicle. On top of that, you might only be one vehicle but you was occupying an entire street's parking space'.

'According to my watch, we were not late'.

'According to my employee you were'.

Uniformed employees with their £signs luminously glowing through the grille crowded around the speaker.

'All right, all right. Gargantua, have you got that money?

Gargantua handed over the cash.

All the £ signs started flashing in unison with the sound of tills crashing open.

'Delusions, delusions, they only exist as long as you're deluded, they are nothing but a stream of conceptual moments. Light does not need another light to see itself. I will not let my mind freeze like ice in delusion. The sun will shine forth.'

Pantagruel spoke to noone in particular.

CHAPTER TWENTY THREE

OF A GREAT QUARREL THAT BROKE OUT BETWEEN THE NERD FOR LIFE FOUNDATION AND £ EMPLOYEES, THE PRIME MINISTER'S SPEECH AND SLIPPERY PAVEMENTS

Gargantua and all were so happy to be in Stinkbomb again and on the road. They booked into The High Park Tower Hotel because the rooms were big enough and settled to a great tea.

'Love the crumpets' Gargantua could not resist.

Pantagruel grunted.

Bigfortydeedee retired, overcome with the exhaustion of the day, whilst the others considered the day's events.

Meanwhile, across town, war was afoot.

News had broken out of a wild sortie of youths, all blonde haired and blue eyed with the countenance of monkeys and with eggs in their right hand and leaflets in their left. They were seen exiting Splash and walking up, down and around the local streets looking for elephant footprints and handing out leaflets

with the speed of a vending machine gone wrong

or an accelerated Tom and Jerry cartoon

or a fruit machine when you strike lucky

or a new fangled photocopier machine emitting a thousand sheets a second

or the power of torrential raindrops

or the flight of the bumblebees.

When approached by the Underworld News Reporter, the youngsters had multifarious explanations:

'We are looking for elephant footprints that will lead us to our master'.

'We are looking for Gargantua. He refused to join us and he must.'

'We must spread the word, our world'.

'There is only one way: our way'.

'We belong to the 'NERDS FOR LIFE FOUNDATION', join us now.'

'Have a leaflet and join us now. We belong to the NERDS FOR LIFE FOUNDATION. Be happy. Enjoy our way of life, the only way of life. Join us now.'

'Are you unhappy? Come and find us: the NERDS FOR LIFE FOUNDATION at your service- eradicate your fears and unhappiness. We are here for you –Now. Your country needs you- Now.'

They spread across L'Undone with organized and efficacious speed, spiders' webs reaching far and wide and leaflet upon leaflet covering pavements until people started to trip on the glossy new surface.

When the original pack of monkeys reached the £, they

were deflected by the luminous signs. Every time they tried to give the £ employees a leaflet, the luminous £ signs would shine so brightly as to blind them. This set off an even stronger determination within the NLF, determination to win . To win whatever. To win at whatever cost. The greater the resistance, the greater the push.

Moreover, the £'s did not just exist in Camedon but at centres all around the City. So as the monkeys spread, hardening in their desire to propagate so too did the £ employees, encouraged by their newly found power.

The employees stepped out and forward, Monopoly paper money leaving the soles of their shoes with every step they took, re-carpeting the pavements with thousands of pounds. From the Old Kent road to Pall Mall, the Strand to Piccadilly and Regent Street to Mayfair, either paper money or shiny slippery glossy leaflets littered the streets.

To boot, since the £ employees were increasingly gaining self-confidence, so too did all the council workers and civil servants as it dawned on them that they were part of one big organization. They took Greater L'undone Counsel. Would the same experience greet their very own leather shoes? The vote was, for the first time in history, unanimous. They chanced it.

Storming out of their stuffy offices, they stomped the streets and to their utter delight, discovered they too were shedding pounds. Slimming Word and Weight Washers watched anxiously.

Pandemonium started to erupt. Hell (or heaven, depending on whose angle you were taking) broke loose. Wires began to get crossed. Mobile phones began to jangle even more than usual.

Crazy monkeys versus £ employees.
Shiny leaflets versus shiny £s.
The blind leading the blind.
Gloss versus Paper.

The government could not fail but to get involved, deploying army tanks at strategic points, generals at the ready with tannoys.

Special announcements were made on television. Neverill Chamberpot, the latest prime minister appeared looking gloomy:

'THIS IS A MESSAGE FROM THE PRIME MINISTER. WOULD ALL PEOPLE PLEASE RETURN HOME. NOW. WE ARE IN A STATE OF EMERGENCY. WE ARE TRYING TO COMMUNICATE WITH TWO PARTIES INTENT ON WAR BUT SO FAR, WE HAVE SIGNIFICANTLY FAILED TO ENTER INTO DIALOGUE.

WE HAVE THEREFORE REACHED LEVEL TWENTY OF TERRORIST ALERT.

FOR YOUR OWN SAFETY PLEASE RETURN HOME NOW.

DO NOT, I REPEAT, DO NOT, PICK UP £S OR GLOSSY LEAFLETS OFF THE PAVEMENTS AND AVOID ALL CONTACT WITH PERPETRATORS' SPIT.'

He continued:

'THE DAY MAY DAWN WHEN FAIR PLAY, LOVE FOR ONE'S FELLOW MAN, RESPECT FOR JUSTICE AND FREEDOM WILL

ENABLE TORMENTED GENERATIONS TO MARCH FORTH SERENE AND TRIUMPHANT FROM THE HIDEOUS EPOCH IN WHICH WE HAVE TO DWELL. MEANWHILE NEVER FLINCH, NEVER WEARY, NEVER DESPAIR.

WARS ARE NOT WON BY EVACUATIONS SO I ASK YOU TO BE STILL. AS SAID PASCAL : 'ALL PROBLEMS ARISE FROM MAN NOT BEING ABLE TO BE IN A ROOM BY HIMSELF.'

LET NO MAN UNDERESTIMATE OUR ENERGIES, OUR POTENTIAL AND OUR ABIDING.'

As soon as this message was played on screen, even more pandemonium broke out.

CHAPTER 24

OF WARTIME MENTALITY, CARPETBAGGERS, STOCKBROKERS, MONEY AND THE LONDON EYE

Collecting £200 as the City brokers passed Go, they all resisted going to jail by throwing the dice three times and buying shares in the Electric Company. Others hurried to get free parking vouchers whilst taking a chance. Others decided to Ritz it out in Piccadilly on Fortnum and Mason sandwiches, pecked at by St.James's Wrens whilst watching the BAFTA awards. Others climbed over high hedges, funding bets by risking jail, avoiding the super tax and hotstepping it to Mayfair and Park Lane. The community chest remained untouched.

But of whichever broker we spoke and from whichever company they came, they had one thing in common: they all spoke on their mobiles at alarming speed.

'Fifty to one- it will settle within the hour.'
'Sixty to two odds on- the monkeys will win'
'One hundred to eleven- the government will obliterate all'
'Five hundred to a half- food will run out'
'Forty to eight- the eggs are the secret weapon'
'Who will place a bet?'
'Do I have your vote?'

'Going to the man in pink in the back row.'

'No to the woman on line 24 from New York for...'

'No to the unknown bidder on the satellite dish...'

'Rien ne va plus.....'

'Ta tat tat a. Ta tat a ta. Ta tat a ta.'

'The ball rolled. The ball rolled some more. Ze ge, zege, zege' (sound of ball rolling)

'The winner is.......'

'Number xxyz23 5945 U.'

'Congratulations. Winner takes all. Would number xxyz23 5945 U please declare himself?'

Meanwhile back in the suite, Gargantua had three televisions on so they had all watched the Prime Minister's appeal.

Pantagruel had joined Bigfortydeedee in the bedroom and sat down to write a letter at the dressing table:

TO GARGANTUA,

'What a sad state the world is that I should bring my family to visit a great capital and inadvertently cause war on a potentially devastating scale.

Gargantua, it is important I return to Singwolf with Bigfortydeedee. She is not as young as she once was and I feel too weary myself to fight a war.

Wars are old-fashioned. In the olden days you could go and war against your neighbour and come back and erect boundaries again. Communities then were independent. War used to solve a problem by destroying the enemy. Your destruction was then your victory. Remember the cake-bakers and Picrochole?

In times gone by, there was pride in joining a war but since Vietnam our attitude has changed.

Nowadays, we are global. Everything is interdependent. When we destroy the neighbours, we destroy ourselves . Walls are no longer possible. The air you breathe in L'Undone affects the butterfly in Yucatan.

We must see the whole world as part of our own body. The concept of war is out of date. It must be dealt with in the modern way.

You, Gargantua, must promote non-violence. You must learn to talk instead of how to solve by force. What use is violence? War is self-destruction.

Talk with respect and compromise.

You should try and remain aware without distraction.

No form, no sound.

L'Undone is an empty house full of bandits. It has eyelashes but cannot see them from its eyes.

'The truth is incontrovertible. Panic may resent it, ignorance may deride it, malice may distort it, but there it is.'

So spoke Churchill in 1916 but although everything changes, the words apply today.

Gargantua, perhaps this is the best education of all for you. Perhaps this is why the war has blown up at this very moment. Perhaps your degree is how to negotiate peace in such turmoil.

Communicate. Talk. Dissolve the war inside your own head. Make friends with your neighbour.

It is all about inner disarmament.

Take care, Gargantua. No son could be more loved by his parents than you are. You have our valiant allies, Dartagne and Zzorroa. They will support you, for sure. Do not forget the Z lineage.'

CHAPTER 25

OF TANNOYS, EGG CONSUMPTION, DRIPS OF WATER AND BROLLIES.

Upon waking Gargantua found his father's letter stuck on the television screen and his parents gone. By now they would be home. A whiff of Singwolf and his idyllic childhood floated past, immediately eradicated by the more pressing and present sound of tannoys in the street.

He opened a window to hear more clearly as Zzorroa and Dartagne appeared dishevelled and rubbing their eyes out of the -same- bedroom.

'HELLO, HELLO. THANK YOU TO THE MAJORITY OF YOU HONOURABLE CITIZENS WHO HAVE STAYED AT HOME.

IT IS OUR UNFORTUNATE DUTY TO INFORM YOU THAT SINCE WE HAVE HAD NO REPLY TO OUR REQUEST TO NEGOTIATE, AND IN CONSEQUENCE OF THIS, WE ARE AT WAR AS OF 11 AM THIS MORNING.

WE WILL NEVER GIVE IN.

YOU ARE ALL REQUESTED TO AVOID THE STREETS AS MUCH AS IS POSSIBLE AND TO CONSIDER YOURSELF ON ENFORCED LEAVE AT HOME.

PLEASE LISTEN TO YOUR RADIOS OR KEEP ABREAST OF THE NEWS ON TELEVISION.

AS BEFORE, PLEASE AVOID
-PAPER MONEY
-SHINY LEAFLETS
-SPIT
AND NOW
-BROKERS GONE MAD FOR A BARGAIN.
YOU VENTURE OUTSIDE AT YOUR OWN RISK.

The television was broadcasting a specialist interview on the subject of eggs.

'Let me give you an example. On average, Mr. Norm in the UK eats about 232 eggs a year. In China they consume 100 per year. But now they have set a target to double the amount of eggs they eat. Since there are 1.3 billion people in China and the population is growing by 14 million people every year, this is quite serious.

Capable Brown has managed to calculate what this would mean. If all the extra chickens were grain-fed, the amount of extra grain needed would be equal to the entire annual export of Australia. Merely to allow China to achieve that relatively minor dietary target would wrap up the total export volume of Australia.

When a nation of 1.3 billion people, growing by 14 million people every year, is expanding its economy faster than any-one in this country would have any capacity to understand, we simply have to come back to the notion of limitations on growth.

'So what do eggs mean to you in view of the current situation?'

'Well, it could mean a number of things. And it would be hard to take a firm view. But if you would like me to put forward my soft-boiled view, it could just be a pot-boiler. Or a foil. Or a symbol. In the past it was the crucifix. Now it could be an egg. Hard-boiled or soft-boiled, that is the question. Will they carry on holding them or will they use them as weapons? Are they past their sell-by date? Are they free range or factory farmed?'

'These are the questions we would like answered but of course nobody is coming forward as their spokesman and what they are saying individually is widely divergent. It is hard to see the pattern behind the words...'

'Yes, of course, there is also some mention of an elephant.'

'Yes indeed but no sighting has yet been made.'

'And some have spoken of a family of giants'

'Ha,ha, ha. Ridiculous, of course. And no confirmation so far'.

'Ah, but we do now have confirmation that there are no eggs left for sale in UK supermarkets. Saintberrry's were the first to sell out, shortly followed by Sadway's and now Weightfell. All the spokesmen are assuring the public not to panic and that they are rushing in fresh stock from abroad. If you look to the sky now, you will see special aeroplanes flying in fresh supplies.'

'Ah, and now we have our leading expert on spit. Professor Water of the Special Institute into Research on Drips of Water, could you please tell us, why do *you* think the government has issued a warning to avoid spit?'

'Well, this of course, is a very interesting matter for debate. We have long been doing research into the rapid descent into madness as a result of ‘your tap left dripping’ syndrome. Nobody can deny the noxious effect this has on one’s brain and it is with this in mind that one concludes that spit is bad for the health. Of course, it naturally depends on what definition of spit one is using. There is the slender bar on which meat that is to be roasted is fixed or the small point of land projecting into the sea or the long and narrow underwater bank. However, on this occasion, and of particular interest to our viewers, it could of course be the ejection of saliva as a sign of hatred or contempt. It could naturally be interpreted as a sign of anger or hostility but could of course refer to the light falling of rain or a fire sending out sparks. This could of course mean the exact counterpart or likeness of these individual monkey like creatures.’

‘Yes, indeed, and moving you forward because we don’t have much airtime left, would you say there is some validity in assuming there is a resemblance to the ‘Stepford Wives’?’

‘Forgive me, that is not my field. I deal solely with the area of water and sensitivity. This has nothing to do with wives and is nowhere near Stepford.’

‘Well, we’ll have to leave it there folks, for today, wishing you all well and

STAY HOME AND DRY!

The cameras focused in on sun shining brightly with presenters holding umbrellas open wide.

‘Time to use your brolly’ made by BrollyCo *was clearly visible on the label.*

CHAPTER TWENTY SIX

OF MODERN DAY WARFARE, FEAR AND LOATHING IN L'UNDONE EYE, VALENTINE, CHAMPAGNE AND WEDDING PROPOSALS

Gargantua watched as did Dartagne and Zzorroa.

'How people have labelled, created and fabricated all out of nothing. How did this all start? And all this less than twenty four hours ago. Where is the reality in it?' Gargantua mused out loud.

A billboard outside flashed : 'Be real, have a coke'.

'It's the dark age we live in, Gargantua' Zzorroa volunteered.

'Not at all. It's not the time nor the age. Time doesn't exist. It's the way we perceive or look at the world that is messy. We are actually in a good position. People aren't bad.'

'That's not what they're saying out there.'

'That's because they all want to blame someone or something. But that only comes from a lack of security. What they need is a sense of freedom. That's what brings about happiness. And no fear. They just don't know how to live day-to-day. Anyway, there's only one way to deal with it and that is to take all this as part of our life. We can't pretend it's not happening.'

'So what are we going to do?' Zzorroa asked.

'Well, as far as I can see, we need to observe what is going on and not get caught up in it. Yes. Let's check our motivation. What do we want to achieve?'

'That's obvious. Peace for all. Stop the nerds getting out of hand', Dartagne offered.

'But now, all the £ employees are joining in.' Zzorroa added nervously.

'Money. It's all about money. It always is somewhere. Money makes the world go around, the world go around that crazy clinking sound of money money money money money money money.' Dartagne started to sing.

The two of them chanted, dancing around the room a la Liza Spinelli and Fred Allstare mixed with a touch of Roger Givememore:

'It's all a cabaret oh chum.'

'Money, it's a crime'

'Money, it's a gas.

Money, so they say.

Is the root of all evil today.'

They fell onto the sofa laughing, pink cheeks from the exertion, floyd running down their arms.

'What is *their* motivation? Is it about money or is it about power? Have the £ employees suddenly realized they have the ability to act?' Gargantua suggested.

Their deep philosophical discussion was interrupted by more tannoy announcements.

'WE ARE ONCE AGAIN ASKING THE POPULATION AT LARGE TO RETURN TO THEIR HOMES.

THE SITUATION IS WORSENING.

NLF MEMBERS ARE TAKING UP POSITION ON THE L'UNDONE EYE. THEY ARE JOINING FORCES AND FORCING THE A&N, RAF, DAD'S ARMY AND LOCAL GROUNDFORCES TO CLOSE DOWN, CALL UP, TAKE UP POSITION OR ABANDON POSITION.

THEY ARE STARTING TO CLIMB ON AND UP THE EYE.

-PLEASE AVOID THE AREA AT ALL COST-

The television screens depicted the same scene: the London Eye lit up in pink, with bottles of vintage, brut, demi-sec, mousseux, Moet and Chandon, Krug, Cristal, Veuve Cliquot and more types of champagne seen clearly advertising their wares and accompanied by signs: 'je t'aime, te quiero, ti amo, ich liebe dich, aishiteru, ya lyoublou tyeba' on billboards, posters, electronic signs and even the carriage windows.

'Whilst all might appear romantic and calm on the Western front, this is truly not so. Valentine's night is indeed a night to celebrate but tonight is not the night. The Nerd for Life Foundation have picked ***this*** *night to converge on the seemingly ideal romantic location: The Eye. The about to be undone in l'Undone I.*

Can you see them? There- One just shot past behind the mast. And another- over there. No the cameras can't seem to catch them but rest assured of this fact: the Nerds are taking over the Eye. It is happening as I stand before you. It is happening as I speak. It is happening. Viewers, this is ...... war......

Now, let's just have a word with the gentleman over here. What can you tell us of the situation inside the Eye? I believe you were actually inside one of the carriages when the Nerds invaded.'

Young, hopeful, pompous and embarrassed man in his late twenties, wearing 100% wool trenchcoat and striped shirt, puts a protective arm around his girlfriend, wearing striped blouse with stiff collar up, string of pearls, hair tied back in a pony tail (the latest fashion to hit Sloane square environs) and green wellies:

'Well, you see, it was like this. I decided to make a romantic proposal to my girlfriend here, Polly Beckwith, and booked a pink carriage in the Eye almost a year ago to the day. That was when I decided that Polly was the one. But then, nervous as you might comprehend that I understandably was, I opened the carriage door for her to climb in when suddenly, out of nowhere, we were assailed by Nerds.'

Polly interrupts:

'Yes, it was terrifying. About fifteen of them. Almost landed on us. Pushed their way into the carriage and pushed us out. Always muttering about us joining them. But we're not nerds and don't wish to be nerds and will never wish to be nerds.'

Turning to her boyfriend:

'Giles, did you mean it? About the proposal? I've been living in hope for the last five years. I was going to dump you if you hadn't decided pretty soon. Don't want to be left on the shelf. Can't hang around forever.'

'Well, you **were** the perfect girl for me. You **were** the one but things have changed now. You might have been infected. So maybe the shelf is the place for you but definitely not hanging around me. Keep away! Got to be so careful nowadays, as you know, don't you know?

And the ring was lost in the melee. Very expensive. Wanted to invest in our future. Suppose I can always claim it back on insurance. That is, if they haven't got a get-out clause.'

Polly dissolves into tears, thumps Giles with her handbag and runs off, breaking her leg as she trips on the leaflets. Two ambulance stretchers are hurriedly brought forward to carry off Giles, unconscious from the blow and Polly, one leg horizontal, one leg straight up in the air.

'Yes, well, let's leave the couple to try and recapture their romance, a shining example of the 'I believe we will get married and live happily ever after' variety 'for better and worse until death do us part'. Let's hope they can find anti-viruses for nerd viruses in the local Accident and Emergency department at the nearby hospital. That's at Land's End, only a six hour drive.

Meanwhile, let us return to the fray. As we speak, more disgruntled passengers are exiting the Eye, whilst desperately trying to avoid slipping on glossy leaflets. Let's go over here to the man in the suit.'

The presenter held forth his mike.

'Sir, Sir, over here. This is LIVE on BBC 10. Could you please tell us what happened to you?'

CHAPTER TWENTY SEVEN

OF THE COMMUTER, CINDY BARBIE AND KEN, BOOBS AND SEX

'Well of course I can tell you about it. It's the same everyday nowadays. They charge you an arm and a leg they do and you just don't get the service. I mean. I get up at four am to get to work now that they've cancelled the six and seven and eight and nine o'clock trains. And then I have to leave at midnight to get home, because they've cancelled the four, five, six, seven, eight and nine pm trains. It then takes me two hours because the train stops at every station and I can't take a nap because if I do, I'll miss my stop. I have to sit blowing on the window and wiping the dirt off the glass to see anything out of the windows because they haven't been cleaned for ten years and then, then, they have the audacity to put the fares up.'

'But Sir, we were trying to get your view on the Nerd situation. Have you not just been ousted by Nerds?'

'Oh, the war. You know to people like me, it's so unimportant. What difference slipping on a few leaflets versus our present quality of life? We're all suffering. Might be a good thing to have a bit of a clear-out. Wouldn't be so squashed on the tube. What's a bit of spit versus somebody's backside in your face every morning? What's a shiny leaflet versus a load of sneezes down your neck? What's a Nerd versus blank faces hidden behind newspapers or Ipods?

And in the grander scheme of things, if it weren't the Nerds or the £s it would be the Nazis or the Communists or Democrat(e)s or some looney group or other pretending they were *really* going to change things '............

He droned on. The presenter, whilst bitterly disappointed that the guy had not spoken about the current situation, showed nothing but a gleaming smile, and, as soon as it was possible, turned the mike to a dolled-up young lady with large bosoms and fuchsia lipstick. She was a bit of all right.

'And what do you think of the situation, Miss?' his eyes darted downwards more often than necessary. *Turning to face the camera directly:*

'Oooh, my name's Cindy Barbie.

Hello mum and dad at home and brother John and auntie Jayne and cousin Tracey and second uncle three times removed, Arthur and grandmother Ethel and granddad Arthur. Ooh, and Mavis down the lane and Tracey up the street.

Waving frantically. Just to let you know I'm safe. In fact, this is my moment of fame. *Turning to the presenter even more directly:* Do you think someone will sign me up for a million £ endorsement now like they all get on Big Brother? Know what I mean?'

The presenter tried to pull the mike away and head off to someone else but the mike seemed to be transfixed to the spot, as did the presenter's gaze. 'What a pair of glorious bosoms, no denying that' he thought to himself.

'No, I haven't had a breast enlargement. They're my own.' Barbie replied volunteering the information as if she had read his mind.

Osmotically, all around the country and all around the globe, the many viewers who had not turned on their televisions, now did so with speed and relish. Branston to be precise. Ratings shot up instantly so that the chairman of the BBC, Lord Losemoney's voice broke into the interviewer's headphones and said:

'Keep her on at all costs. If she goes, so does your job. She's filling up our coffers and we need the pounds or we'll all lose our jobs'.

The interviewer got the message and was actually quite pleased by the enforced need to keep the mike close to so splendid a pair.

'Boobs. If we lose boobs, we've lost the world, let alone the war. The world seems to be fixated on boobs and Viagra. Been on the net recently? I get 300 emails a day offering wonderful bargains.'

The interviewer started to perspire slightly.

'Does this not bother you, being on television and talking about he hem...*(he coughs nervously)?*'

She interrupts:

'Sex. You must be joking! If men are meant to be thinking about it every six minutes, I assure you women are thinking about it just as frequently if not more. Love it. Do it all the time. In fact, I was looking for my boyfriend when you arrived. He's called Ken Schagger and has a red sports car. Have you seen him?'

'No, I'm afraid I haven't but I'm sure somebody will spot him now you're on television. So coming back to the point, that is, not the war, but ...Viagra...(with a capital because it's so important, interjects the author, since the keyboard will not let it type without, must be its sacred position in society)....doesn't it bother you that you're bombarded with boobs, Viagra and sex?'

'Not at all. What else is there?'

'Well, serious matters like work, the state of the world, property prices and so forth...'

'Why are those important? What is more important than sex? Saturday night, get a vid or DVD, bottle of wine, Gstrings and Boob's your uncle. Oh no, love, you've got a problem if you think there's more important than sex. Why else is it so wide-spread on the net? Why else is it taking over our emails? That's the real world. Forget about Nerds. Sex will be there a long time after they've gone. Sex has to be there. This isn't called reality TV for nothing. You might judge but you don't know nothing.

Ooh, there's my Ken. Now just look at all that muscle. Hey girls, hands off, he's mine. But isn't he just so ... (licking of lips) ....fit?'

Cameras turn to big hunk, black mane, tight jeans and large bulges on each arm and elsewhere, leaving red sports car parked on pavement and rushing towards Cindy Barbie with aplomb. They hug, passionately and ardently kiss before the cameras, her perfect lipstick leaving marks across his face.

'Tiger' she cooed.

'Honey' he replied, breathless and brandishing 24 red roses with gypsophilia.

His hands ventured over her derriere as she pummelled his

chest with her protrusions.

The presenter's hand started to shake as he was forced to move back to make way for them whilst still keeping his focus.

'Honey' Ken repeated.

'Oooohhhhh' Cindy Barbie gasped.

'What to do?' thought the presenter. To lose my job and move on or to lose my job and stay put? That is the question. 'Keep going, talk your way out of it' he thought.

'Well, here you can see a shining example of stiff upper lip. Not conceding to fear in the face of war. In fact, completely ignoring the enemy and engaging in sexual activity. Contrary to popular complaints, it seems to be working for them. Perhaps this is our armour. Take up sex and defeat the enemy. After all, the world might end today and then where would we be? In fact, maybe Cindy Barbie and Ken have made an important point. If the world were to end today at one, where would you most liked to have been? In bed of course. So might I take it upon myself, your BBC presenter, Playedsafe Untiltoday, to recommend that the best known antidote to war to date is SEX.'

Cameras zoom in on Cindy Barbie and Ken getting rather heated. Moans of pleasure become noisier. Mr Playedsafe Untiltoday clearly getting a little hot under the collar, hand distinctly shaking as he holds the mike as close to them as possible. Unable to keep upright, Ken lays Cindy Barbie on the ground on a nest of glossy leaflets.

Mr. Playedsafe Untiltoday leans down as far as he can without falling on top of them.

Suddenly he regained his senses. What was more likely to

create a problem? Sex or glossy leaflets?

A large hand on his shoulder pulled him up.

'Here, enough sex, it's not past the nine o'clock watershed. Think of the kids watching this. Now talk to *me*, I can tell you the latest.'

CHAPTER TWENTY EIGHT

OF GYMNAST, ON YOUR BIKE, SCENES OF DEVASTATION AND BROKEN LEGS, MORE NERDS AND MORE SEX, CROSS OUT, LOVE. DO NOT SWITCH OFF. IMAGINE.

'Stupid idiots, those guys. That will be the end of them, I guarantee. It's not all about sex, they've got it wrong. They're addicted to sex. It's a rush they need. Think. Just one thought can give you an erection. Just one thought. So many thoughts all directed to sex. They've definitely got it wrong....

Actually, I'll let you into a little secret...: it's all about keep-fit. Or maybe that's if you haven't got the sex. Or maybe, like me, it could be about both. My name's Fonder by the way. I came here on my trusty stead.

Cameras point to bicycle rideometerspectacular machine, Olympics 2006 Nought On. Tour de France via l'Undone.

'It's quite clear what's going on. Some idiots or nerds have got too big for their boots and they're being shot down by £s. But what they all need is exercise. Now watch this.

With marvellous strength and agility, Fonder twirled to the left and the right. When he had done this he put his right-hand thumb upon the bow of the seat, raised himself up and sprung in the air, poising and upholding his whole body upon the muscle and nerve of the said thumb, and so turned and whirled himself about three times. At the fourth, reversing his body, and overturning it upside down, and fore-side back, without touching anything, he brought himself betwixt the two handlebars, springing with all his body into the air, upon the thumb of his left hand, and in that posture, turning like a windmill, did do a full turn. After this, clapping his right hand flat upon the middle of the seat, he gave himself such a jerking swing, that he thereby seated himself upon the crupper, after the manner of gentlewomen.

This done, he easily passed his right leg over the seat and placed himself upon the crupper. 'But' he said, 'it would be better for me to sit down' then putting the thumbs of both hands on the crupper before him and leaning against it, he turned heels over head in the air, and found himself straight sitting in a comfortable position. Then, with a somersault, springing into the air again, he fell to stand with both his feet close together on the seat and there twizzled round more than a hundred times, with arms held out across; so doing he cried out aloud: 'I rage, I rage... ‘I rage, I rage, I rage against flab. I rage against the non-fit. I rage against producers of full-fat milk. I rage against chocolate. I rage against couch potatoes.’

Enraged and all the rage in fashion, ironically his I pod popped out of his inside anorak tracksuit pocket. Using the earplug wires as weapons, he lassooed them with strength to the top of one of the Eye’s carriages and hoisted himself up in hot pursuit. He then repeated his morning exercise routine as described on the last page and threw himself at the window of one of the carriages. Spread-eagled against the window, he stuck out his tongue and waggled it long and hard against the glass, doing much the same exercise as his whole body had on the bike, whilst spelling the sign 'Nerds, go home' on the wind-screen with his fingers.

It was impossible to get a close-up of the Nerds but their shadow seemed to shrink or maybe they were even crouching down inside. Unfortunately, the act of tongue-wagging and the force of his anger spent, he slid irrevocably to the ground where yet more stretchers were needed to withdraw him with two broken legs arched backwards in arabesque style.

At this point, Played Safe Untiltoday had had enough. He started stamping the ground and champing at the bit.

'I simply can't carry on with this report. I want to go home. I want to make love.'

Turning to a complete stranger on his left he asked:

'Come home with me and make love? Making love is all there is to do. Sexual healing. I want you, now, baby. Make luv, listen to the music'.

Camera focuses on pretty woman.

'My name is Yosho. Let's go'.

Playedsafe Untiltoday set the camera and mike to auto record as they sang in unison:

'Imagine there's no heaven
It's easy if you try
No hell below us
Above us only sky
Imagine all the people

Living for today...
Imagine there's no countries
It isn't hard to do
Nothing to kill or die for
And no religion too
Imagine all the people
Living life in peace...
You may say I'm a dreamer
But I'm not the only one
I hope someday you'll join me
And the world will be as one
Imagine no possessions
I wonder if you can
No need for greed or hunger
A brotherhood of man
Imagine all the people
Sharing all the world...
You may say I'm a dreamer
But I'm not the only one
I hope someday you'll join us
And the world will live as one.'

They kissed for all the world to see and walked off in the crepuscular dusk heading for peace and love.

But at that very moment the brokers, touts or wheeler-dealers arrived, blocking the newly loving couple's departure and the wonderful view of the Thames with the words:

'Give us £2000 immediately for using those lyrics or you will not pass go. We will sue you for using such famous words without copyright permission. Pay up immediately or go to jail. Now.'

It just so happened that 2000 £ employees were deploying before their very eyes.

'How timely. There's your payment' Mr. Played Safe Untiltoday pointed behind him. The brokers glanced away for a second allowing him to whisk Yosho away, elegantly skating along the leaflets.

He would play safe no more.

CHAPTER TWENTY NINE

OF THE PRIME MINISTER AND THE SWORD AND DEVASTATION

The Prime Minister was back on the screen as Gargantua and co still kept watch.

A new presenter in the studios attacked:

'And what do you say, Prime Minister about the current situation?'

Focus on Prime Minister quietly chatting to the sound engineer, blissfully unaware he was being broadcast across the globe in errata.

'Lovely buns that girl had, didn't she? Wonder if she will get an endorsement. Otherwise, I might have to have a private word with her. ChamberpotClintgate and all. That was about having sexual relations or not having sexual relations. That was the question. Making love or not making love, *that* is the question today'.

Without drawing breath he carried on, looking the camera straight in the eye.

' If we fail, then the whole world, including the United States, including all that we have known and cared for, will sink into the abyss of a new Dark Age made more sinister, and perhaps more protracted by the lights of pervert science. Let us therefore brace ourselves to our duties and so bear ourselves that, if the United Kingdom, indeed the world, last for a 1000 years, men will say: ‘this was your finest hour’.

‘But Prime Minister, those may be fine words, but the question related not to the war but to the people’s comments. Will commuting ever improve? Will you ever mean what you say? Should we all go home and make love? Let’s have a look at this blackboard for example. On here you will see quotations that your government has made over the last five years. And now look what a pickle we’re in. Branston again. What we need is Branson. Virgin would sort it out.’

‘I never said these things’ Chamberpot replied.

‘Not you directly, but members of your party certainly did. Prophetic almost, don’t you think, number 6 especially? Not number 10. And now it’s all blowing up in our faces.’

‘Not our faces. No blowing up. Just our feet and a lot of broken legs. Too many. Time to show what we are truly made of. And it’s not just legs. Nor is it puppy dogs tails, nor is it sugar and spice. We’ll show them our mettle. Our gold, silver, copper, iron, lead, tin, aluminium or uranium. We will show them our holographic chemicals. We are all nerve cells wired together to create identity’.

‘This is not what people want to hear, Sir, with all due respect. They want results.’

‘And that’s what we’ll give them, don’t you worry. You see, with all due respect, your view is biased. However, I absolutely love your camera. Look at it. It looks at the board. It looks at me. It looks at everything. It sees more than just me because it has no judgement. It is not obscura’.

Back at the tower, Gargantua cheered:

'That is the first time I've heard him say anything true. Wonderful. Wonder what happened to him. 'Science sans conscience n'est que ruine de l'ame'. So said Rabelais, I believe. Now. Things are heating up a little too much. I don't really want to show my face if I can avoid it, because it might cause even more anxiety. But please, adjutants, to the fore.'

Zzorroa and Dartagne had been dying to take action and

1. 'Vote for us because we believe in and will always react to fear, like our special friends'

2. 'Vote for us because we will bring in measures to accelerate global drunkenness, and consumption of harsh addictive intoxicants. We WANT to encourage pollution and carbon gas emissions because we can't see beyond the end of our noses. Our descendants will look after themselves'

3. 'Vote for us because_we ***know*** *we know it all and that you don't'.*

4.'Vote for corruption'.

5.'Vote for us because we will take all your money and misspend it again and again'.

6.'Vote for us for a SAFE democracy (the small print notes: when you wear gas masks, bullet proof vests, bomb detectors and stay in at all times.)

7.'Vote for us because secretly, and we are letting you into a very big secret, we don't know what to do and don't really care as long as we are in POWER.'

8.'Vote for us because we believe in might and can squash all terrorism. We KNOW! TRUST US! We have the answers.'

were delighted by the encouragement. Gargantua was turning more and more into his father by the second.

'Let's go straight for the Z Foundation as planned. That was what Pantagruel was intimating, after all.' Zzorroa leapt up.

Author's interjection:

Now some of you might still be wondering, dear readers, why, a few chapters ago, they had both appeared looking dishevelled out of the same bedroom.

Some of you might have been day-dreaming about the start of a true love affair. You might have spent time imagining their lingering first kiss when you put down this un-putdown-able tome to pop to the loo.

Others among you, go on, admit it, might have been fancying they were at it, like wild rabbits. And your thoughts might have become a little heated.

Whilst the cynics among you might have decided it was all far too predictable.

Well, I hate to disappoint you, but the fact is it was the only spare bedroom and it did have twin beds. With sleep a necessity, common sense prevailed and a room was shared with all propriety.

Dartagne, always the gentleman, had kept his back turned to Zzorroa and Zzorroa out of desperate desire to deter desire, had kept her back to Dartagne.

B U T !! this is what truly happened, for to lie would be against my principles.

In the middle of the night, they had both had dreams....

Zzorroa had dreamt that jiffying the streets of L'Undone, she had bumped into the infamous large elephant all the Nerds were looking for and had slayed him. She had jumped on his hump and dashed him with the swish of a Z, thus causing the elephant to have the hump and fall down vanquished.

Meanwhile Dartagne had dreamt that he was walking up a rounded raised mass of earth or hump when he was suddenly landed on by an elephant. He got the hump. But once over the hump, which was only momentary, he found himself in the arms of an attractive Humpty Dumpty who suggested they humped. Never one to enjoy a lady, or in this case egg, to take the lead, he got the hump once again. And so they didn't hump. Rather Humpty Dumpty turned into a humped back whale. Dartagne scrabbled around and reaching for his sword started to swish the whale.

At this very point, the 'couple' both woke up to find themselves on top and beneath each other, legs and arms all over the place, hands empty as if holding swords and about to slay each other. Both were extremely embarrassed, yelled 'humph!!!!!' and fell onto their separate beds in shock.

Was it a wonder that their hair looked dishevelled the following morning?

And the author must further add that she was distraught upon discovering that in the last five hundred years a character called Lewis Carroll had usurped her Rabelaisian rights to play with words in the 'Looking Glass', allowing humpty dumpty to make words mean what he chose. Rabelaise, too was in a hump.

CHAPTER THIRTY

OF SYMBOLS, TIES, Z, SOUVENIRS AND TEXTING

Dartagne had a hunch about the hump and discussed its meaning with Zzorroa.

'The symbol is quite clear. The egg and the elephant were clear attacks and we both resorted to swords to slay the enemy'.

'Except of course that there was no blood and you didn't actually use yours, you just started to.'

'Exactly'.

'You had better watch out for your tie' Zzorroa added.

'What's wrong with me wearing a tie?'

'Thought you'd missed it. It was on the news an hour ago. 'Wear a dirty tie and you become a killer!' they said. 'Apparently, lurking in the threads of a dirty tie lie a host of unpronounceable bugs including methicillin-resistant staphylococcus aureus, c.difficile, streptococcal bacteraemia, enterococcus bacteraemia, acinetobacter bacteraemia, e faecimum and fungal candida. Don't you see? If you get a dash of spit or a bit of egg on it, you could inadvertently infect instead of cure. It could of course be that this is the secret enemy....It so happens that the earliest known necktie was found in the mausoleum of China's first emperor, Shih Huang Ti who was buried in 210 BC.... Later Louis XIV of France was intrigued by the colourful silk kerchiefs worn around the necks of Croatian mercenaries. But it is also said ties come from the word cravate from the land Croat. As long ago as 1660, King Charles II who had spent years of exile in France returned to England and the new craval was suddenly all the rage.

And they all had relationships with elephants.'

'Thanks for that. Zzorroa. I will take heed. Now, shall we go?'

Having attached new jiffy bags to their feet with rope, they glided across L'Undone, heading for the Z Foundation. The streets were deserted except for a few lone Nerds walking by, in a manner reminiscent of the Stepford Wives.

'They only need to be pricked to change their tune' Dartagne said.

'Now that's an idea...

Anyway, we've almost reached the Z centre. I wonder if anyone's around?'

The Z centre was situated on the corner of Trafalgar Square, where Lyons Corner house had once been. Normally people gathered around by their thousands but for now, only lone Nerds and a few Pounds were present.

The building was modelled in three dimensions which helped to accommodate the lack of shear walls or braced cores. Instead structural support relied on joint stiffness for stability. The vast entrance to the site was the result of an impressive 20 metre cantilever from the reinforced concrete core. This provided a spatially dramatic entrance. Security consultants' expertise in blast resistant design and façade specialists advised on windows and cladding elements such as granite, slate, timber and pre cast concrete to reduce hazard to occupants in the case of a bomb blast.

The door opened automatically as they approached allowing them to walk into the splendid ante-room. This was empty and the ticket booths closed. They put some money on the counter and jumped over the automatic entrance gates.

Heading for the souvenir shop, they found what they were looking for: their choice weapons: two swords and shields. Even if they were made of plastic.They hurriedly left more money on the counter and pulled off the cellophane wrapping.

Rushing outside before they fell asleep, they skated past the fountain when out of the blue (more blue), a beautiful lady's voice could be heard emanating from seemingly nowhere.

'Why did you not try your hand at the sword?' the voice asked.

So bizarre and unexpected a question, that Zzorroa and Dartagne replied at the same time:

'Because it's not likely to be us in a million years'

'Because we're not likely to be the one in a million'

'But this story goes back more than a million years, my children, and always there is cause and effect. Every action has a reaction and this has led you two to this very spot and this very point. The question is what will you do with this spot? Will you run on or face the truth of your destiny? Truth or dare? The winner takes all.'

'Who are you to speak to us this way?' Dartagne enquired.

'And even you to' Zzorroa added.

'I am the Lady of the Fountain. A bit stirred and definitely shaken, I have waited rather a long time for this moment. *You are the one*. Please go and fulfil your destiny.'

Dartagne and Zzorroa looked around searching for the source of the voice. Dartagne thought he could see a transluscent mermaid with beautiful long hair emanating from the water but wondered if it might be the advertisement billboard flashing in the background with 'Martini' and 'Opium' and 'MORE' written in large across it. He looked at Zzorroa, they grinned and without hesitation, headed back through the magnificent entrance.

Further down by the riverside, 1666 brokers appeared. All textmessaging.

Tstmsg extraordinaire.

Milton's Paradise Lost in tstmsg:

'Devl kikd outat hevn coz jelus of jesus&strts war.pd'off wiv god so corrupts man(me by god) wiv apel.devl stays serpnt 4hole life&man ruind. Woe un2mnkind.'*

Two to one, they can't do it.

What was that?

'The learning opportunities afforded by text messaging have so far been underexploited'.

Three to four.

'MadwyfSetsFyr2Haus'

Spot the book.

'Jane Eyre, of course'.

'Indeed. Fifty to one you get the next one'.

'FeudTween2hses-Montague&Capulet. RomeoM falls<3w/-JulietC@marySecretly BtR killsJ'sCoz&is banishd.

J fakes Death. As part of Plan2b-w/R Br-leter Bt IT Never Reachs Him. Evry 1 confuzd-both Luvrs kil Emselves'.*"

'Will they or will they not draw the sword?'

A thousand to one they won't and will it be him or will it be her? To be continued.....

*1He is angry with God and so corrupts man (who is made by God) with an apple. The devil remains as a serpent for the whole of his life and man is ruined. Woe unto mankind.'

*2 A feud between two houses- Montague and Capulet. Romeo Montague falls in love with Juliet Capulet and they marry secretly but Romeo kills Juliet's cousin and is banished. Juliet fakes her own death. As part of the plan to be with Romeo she write him a letter but it never reaches him. Everyone is confused and both lovers kills themselves.'

CHAPTER THIRTY ONE

OF AUTOMATED PHONE CALLS, ARTHUR, ECEPHRON AND THE READER HAVING TO WAIT

The brokers tried to speak to the newspapers, television and anyone who would gamble but there was a problem. Not an unusual one. It went like this:

Thank you for calling. We do not wish to keep you waiting. In order to provide you with an efficient service, press 2 and then 2 again. When you have done this, you might get straight through or you might be ten in line. The expected waiting time is fourteen days and five minutes. Press 5 and then hold. Option one means you will never get through to us. Option two means you will be asked some security points, lasting no more than five hours. These involve such soul-searching questions that you will be put through to our further security department to be reminded of the answers to your secret questions. *Who was your first love?* has proved a tricky one for most of our clients. As does *what was your mother's name?*

At this point many people get 'accidentally' cut off.

Option three means you will then press 1 then 2 then 5. The reason this is taking so much time is that we have decided it is a good way to run a foreign language course. Whilst waiting for the main reason for your call, you could press Z and then 10 for our new range of *'learn Zabadoudou whilst holding on. In our day and age, time is money. Don't lose out.*

**there will be a small charge for this service that will be added to your bill. Only £2.50 with taxes of 90%'.*

Option four allows you to hear what a wonderful company we are. This is enforced listening time because if you have got this far, hanging up is just a little too unbearable to consider. Too much shame involved. That feeling that you are getting old and are a technophobe. That feeling that your children could get through standing on their head. That feeling that it is only your incompetence stopping success. Guilt. Impatience. Anger. Pride.

There is no other option. Starting again is only for fools. Listen instead to how perfect we are and be brainwashed.

Option five leads to section 1,2,3, and 4. When you press 4, you will disconnect automatically. We are doing all this so that we don't have to provide expensive staff to answer what will undoubtedly be an abusive call about the paucity of our service or a stupid call for which you did not need to ring and bother us.

'Hello, hello,' the brokers yelled mercilessly. 'Is anyone there?'

At last, Mr. Grotty Perotti from HLM (the Height of L'Undone Madness Bank- incidentally, the tallest building in Europe at 90 storeys high- After all once you've gone 10 or 12 storeys, another 80 won't make that much difference) got through.

'Am I really through to someone?' he asked unbelievingly.

Ten minute gap before the reply reaches him.

'Of course, sir, you are through to Ahmed in Bombay.'

‘But I want some action here in l’Undone right now.’

‘Sir, please do not raise your voice. I can promise you a velly excellent service if you will just answer these questions first.’

‘But I’ve been through this two hours ago.’

‘I’m velly velly sorry Sir but it is part of our company’s policy. I cannot proceed without you giving me this information.’

Grotty Perotti interrupted in haughty voice, intent on reporting the lousy employee:

‘Can you tell me who you are?’

‘Yes, Sir, I am level three.’

‘AAAAAAAAhhhhhhhhh’ Grotty Perotti threw down his mobile in despair, his mind boggled. His was not the only one. All the brokers were encountering the same problem.

This was of course a rather handy diversion, permitting Dartagne and Zzorroa to have free rein inside the Foundation. Using straps attached to their bodies and rope they sprinted up the vertical wall, being reeled in by a pulley-like device like a fish on a line as they climbed. They were rigged with a decelerator, a hydraulic device to slow them down but they free-fell for 60 feet before it kicked in, and it was an abrupt stop. They would have messed up pretty badly if anything had gone wrong. It was just like a Cruise in the Vatican. Definitely a nigh on impossible mission.

And so they were in....

And there before them was ......

THE SWORD IN THE SHAPE OF A Z

tucked into a huge granite boulder.

Above it was an extract from the Stories of King Arthur's Knights:

'Then Merlin told him to look out over the lake and when he did so he saw a hand rising from the water and holding in its grasp a beautiful sword.

'If you speak to the lady of the lake,' Merlin said, 'she will perhaps give it to you.' So King Arthur spoke to the beautiful girl, and she told him that if he would promise to give her what she asked, whenever she asked it, he should have the sword. Arthur promised and the lady disappeared; and the king rowed out in her boat and took the sword from the hand which came out of the water. And the sword was called Excalibur and was very beautiful and powerful.'

'Which one of us is the one?' Zzorroa asked.

'I have no idea but you go first, since you're the lady.' Dartagne said.

Zzorroa looked at the sword's handle. She spat on her hands for luck and laughed. Breathing deeply, she grabbed it. Nothing moved.

'It must be you then' she turned to Dartagne, yawning strongly and falling into a bundle of sleep on the ground.

Dartagne moved up to the sword swiftly and tried to remove it but with no more success than Zzorroa. He too fell asleep in a heap.

On top of her. Again.

Would they wake up? Would they manage to withdraw the sword? Was it all a mistake to stop them going forward? Would they make it out before the world found out?

Among those present was Mr.Wiseguy who said: 'It's like the story of Mr. Rainyday who saved all his pennies and hid them under the floorboard. He spent moment after moment thinking of the day he would retire.

He dreamt of
not going to work anymore,
of the delicious cocktails he would drink
of the sexy women he would chat up
and the lazy days he would spend
lying on a sunlounger
on a white sandy beach
looking up at never-ending blue skies....

On the day he had calculated as having exactly the right amount necessary, it just so happened that a neighbour's son blew up his own and Mr.Rainyday's house in an accidental chemistry experiment...All his money blown to smithereens. ... Not only that, beaches were declared unsafe zones owing to global warming and alcohol banned in all public places.

For more of this and other stories, please tune in tomorrow - same time, same place.

CHAPTER THIRTY TWO

OF METALL G. BILL, INVESTMENTS, WI, RESISTANCE

Back at the ranch or the Eye or the I or the aille aille aille or the 'Ay, ay, ay, what's going on there' ay, the Nerds had completely taken over the Wheel. Pound employees had poured in and were grouped behind the various ticket offices. After a few in-fights, their leader had become self-evident: Metall G. Bill, known for his ruthless amassing of millions if not trillions over the last decade, master of the deal and of government stocks, decided it was time to speak up.

Being a self-publicist he grabbed the abandoned television camera, pointed it at himself and got some employees to start filming.

'Hello everyone back home. At last, I can talk some sense. Perhaps it is time for you to take in what most of you have avoided all your life.

Life is a risk and just like snakes and ladders has a risk/reward spectrum- a scale along which all investments might be arrayed. You can try

spread-betting where you will lose most of your money
or options, a contract that gives you the right to buy
or sell an investment at a specified price in the future.
Penny would go for small-cap shares

whilst high-flyers, wearing their caps in the middle of their heads hedge on blue-chip shares.

You might prefer to find a tracker to actively manage your funds or lend your money to corporate bounders.

Our Pound employees have all invested in guilt, cash Eyesis or Is As or Eyes As in the Post Office National Savings or cash deposited in banks and buildings. That is our society.

The £ or POUND.

We have been telling you for many years of the advantage of our product but most of you have chosen to ignore us.

'The mass of men lead lives of quiet desperation' wrote Henry Thoreau. Many triggers make us desperate, none more powerful than money or the lack of it. Serious financial problems are leading to divorce, depression and death.

Yet the truth is that good money management skills can be simple and straightforward for the majority of people. If you had assets like mine, your finances would be complicated but you don't. What you worry about is if your washing machine starts leaking or your boiler goes on the blink or -worst of all- your television breaks down. No, worse than that, no money for fags or booze. What to do then if you have had no forethought? Money buys you choices. It is no more-no less important than that. Listen to our refrain:

What the world needs now, is money sweet money.
Please sing along and see the error of your ways.
Put on the pounds and save the pounds
But don't buy foreign, specially sprouts
Beware euromania 'cos It's phoney.

What the world needs now, is more money sweet money.

The BBC managed to pick up the amateur broadcast and sent extra crew to the area. It was hard to find interviewers willing to go so close to enemy territory and naturally involved large sums of - money.

Meanwhile, leading experts on finance were hurriedly tanked into the studio.

Mr Right from the 'Live Right and support the world Foundation' spoke:

'How incredibly typical. They only think of what's in front of their noses, their home and the weight in pounds they've put on- they can't even go metric. They do not even stop to consider the global situation. Africa for example.'

'Well, we have had examples like Live aid and so forth. And many people go to Asia and other exotic locations for facelifts.'

'Indeed but they need to realize that quick fixes don't exist- if there were magic bullets, it is reasonable to assume they would have identified and deployed them by now'

'Please don't bring up the subject of bullets. It might prove dangerous in the circumstances'

'Indeed, but we need to invest in governance, accountability and transparency in government and be prepared to play very hard ball when these are not forthcoming.'

'Perhaps balls are a dangerous notion, right now as well.'

'Indeed, but one other pertinent point. Given that the Indian sub-continent is home to twice as many very poor (less than a dollar a day is the world bank's standard definition) people as the entire African continent....why all the fuss about Africa alone?'

'Please don't set off another war. We see what you are trying to say, clearly, this is a global matter and we are all caught up in our own country. The thing is, isn't that always the way?'

'It has been but can no longer remain so. Your previous speakers have already discussed this. You might consider why the press doesn't devote more than a millimetre of print to major annual catastrophes like flooding in Bangladesh. Is that conditioned by finances as well? Are you all puppets to Metall G. Bill? If I were you, I would look deeper into what that man is made of. Has he paid his bills? Is he really hard metal? What does the G stand for? Has he met all and got Grand bills?

Anyway I need to get on with my work. I don't have time for dilly dallying talking about it. Either you're part of the problem or part of the solution. Onwards and upwards. You might have a war here but it is so insignificant in the bigger plan. Soon the £ will no longer exist. Where is Europe after all? Why should we think ourselves so different? So separate? We are part of Europe, part of the world. And as for the I, very ephemeral indeed.

The reporter interrupted to screen a few thousand WI members heading straight to the Eye, brollies in hand. They pushed Metal G Bill out of the way. It was hard not to notice them, for brolly apart, they were sporting (such was their voluminous weight and fortitude), tin bras with mini swords sticking out as extensions to their nipples. Dangerous to hug them. Their leader was particularly fierce with tight-fitting Marks Expensive 100%new wool jumper, scratchy tweed skirt, brown stockings and brown Kshoes. Mrs. I Willbeherd grabbed the microphone and spoke:

'We are the largest body of women in England and whilst some of us are already digging bunkers to hide in and stockpiling food, most of us are of this opinion. We need to get away. We need somewhere safe from germs. We need to fly away. Get the government to put on extra cheap flights. Ban the taxes and let us take flight now. I bet their eggs are not biodynamic organic. We believe in truth, justice, tolerance and fellowship. We care about climate change and environmental degradation. We need to conserve our resources. That said, fly us out and stop flying more eggs in. Open our airports.

Fly, fly away in my beautiful, my beautiful machine.

Fly away home.

Fly Laker later.

There are only 215000 of us. We are mere flies in the ointment.

Fell I . Fell I. Fell eye. Fell I. It's all f-lies. Fell -a- show. Sorry, that's my private thoughts.

Air is the remedy. Fresh air. Open your windows. Nobody does nowadays. It will be a rinse-out. In and out like a fiddler's elbow.

Join the resistance.

Ladies of the WI, unite. Ladies who have not yet joined, join now!

We wear our suit of armour with pride.

CHAPTER THIRTY THREE

OF MIRRORS, GALILEO, REAL LIFE, BUCKINGHAM PALACE, ANONYMITY AND ELEPHANTS

Gargantua was wondering how Dartagne and Zzorroa were getting on. Getting on or getting on? Getting it on? Getting on it? Getting? Getting it? Or getting off?

He was itching to sort it all out but to scratch the itch would bring about consequences. Best to sit with the itch.

It would be the end of his anonymity.

He took a shower and prepared himself. He checked his mind. He checked the mirror. He looked at his image in the mirror. Did he really look like that? Was that really him? Never! It was the same as the reflection of the moon in water. Would anyone dive into the water and take out the moon? The mirror misted up. A good thing.

He was distracted. It felt like carrying water in his hands.

He inspired. One. Inspiration counts. Two. After a few minutes he directed his inspiration to others. Three. Four. Five. Billions.

He watched the television once again. It all seemed to be taking place around the same quarter. The London Eye,

Perhaps he should write to the President or the Queen. He laughed. He picked up a few tourist brochures on the desk.

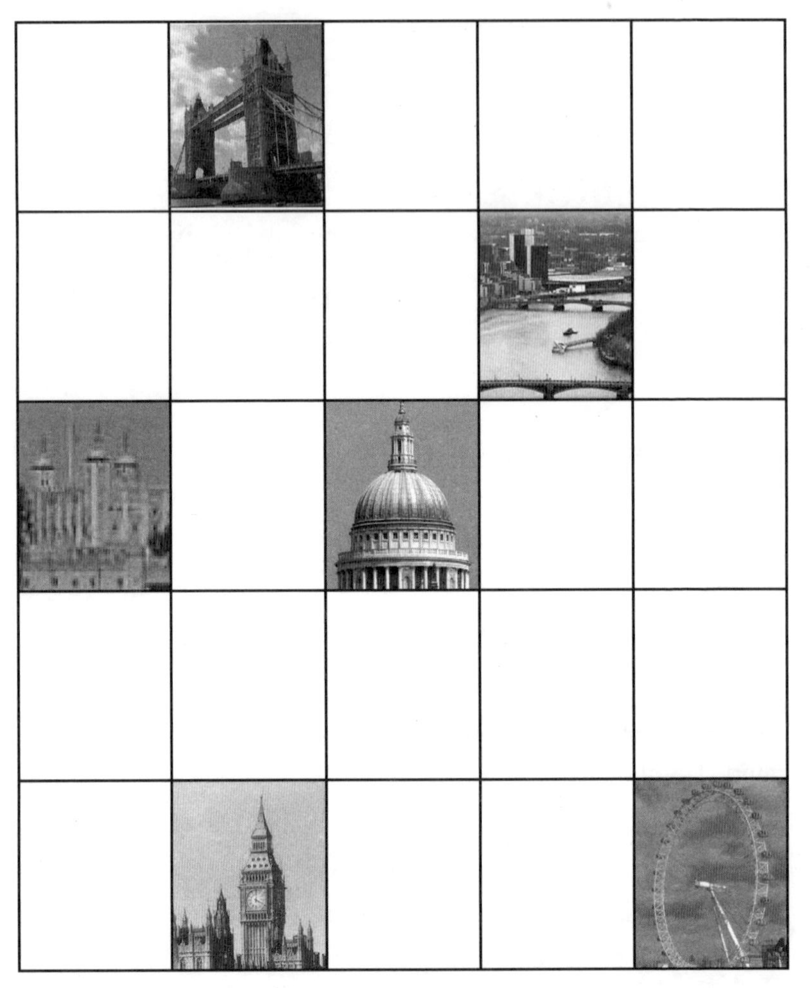

Madame Tussaud's. Buckingham Palace. The Tower of London. That's where he should go. Pay a little visit to his old friends. Do a little sight-seeing?

He felt strangely sleepy.

Of course! They must have fallen asleep. That's why he was finding it hard to concentrate. Dangerous stuff. Time to get a move on.

He stood up and walked down the staircase into the street

and climbed into Stinkbomb. It was important to slow his actions down because he was engaging in activity. He drove slowly down the Mall, past the Palace.

Ignoring government warnings, The Queen was having a garden party. She was not for moving out. She was still reigning but not ruling. Let them get on with it. She had seen enough wars to not be intimidated. Her show must go on. But she had not allowed for her guests being replaced with Nerds. The Nerds had conspired to steal invitations and arrived en masse. They were *everywhere*, just like an ant infestation, eggs in hand and spitting.

The Queen still considered duty before everything and it was her duty to serve.

Luckily, she had not accounted for Gargantua's machine either.

Needing to refuel, he pressed on the F button and a hose, much resembling an octopus's tentacle or a hoover or, let's be British, a Dyson's arm was ejected which automatically sniffed out the required combustion and therefore immediately swept over the Palace Walls and sucked up the 27000 cups of tea, 20 000 sandwiches and 20 000 slices of cake set out on the lawn on the 408 foot long buffet. It was naturally premium quality which was good for his car and since it belonged to the common wealth, Gargantua felt within his rights. It might improve their development, democracy, debt management and trade.

The band was left playing the National Anthem, the Queen retained her smile and the guests were left, arms holding nothing, in the air.

'It must be a cut back.'

'Is this for real?'

'Last minute rationing'

'We are at war after all.'

'Or is this a fantasy?'

'Well, *there's no escape from real life'*

'Reality says we should be at home'

'But given a choice between Queen and Country, the Queen has my vote.'

'She is a champion.'

'No, we are all champions.'

'The Mother of them all.'

'Mama mia'.

'Shame about the food, though. You would have thought she would have known better'

'After all, the Queen had had well over a million people to tea.'

'Maybe the 400 staff weren't enough to deal with the 8000 guests?'

'I'm just a poor girl, from a 2.2 family.'

'Nothing really matters to me'

'Oh, war is *very frightening'*

'Remember, Galileo?'

'But it's still *magnifico*'.

'Is that his measurement of fallen bodies?'

Pointing to an antique garden gnome in the shape of Albert.

'Do heavier objects fall faster than lighter ones?

'Like thunder and lightning'

'More like lighter ones fly into aspirators'.

The Queen was a little battle weary. Why oh why did that

machine have to aspirate food? Why did it not aspirate her guests? Could it not have been more thoughtful? Could it not have sucked up the 3 million items of correspondence she had dealt with or the 387 700 awards and honours she had yet to confer? Now this might get out to the 200 million viewers around the world. The inconvenience of it all. Not how it used to be.

The grass is always greener. Her grass was definitely greener. But what she would give for anonymity. Her face gave away nothing. Did anyone enjoy their fame? Did Shakespeare enjoy being locked up writing his plays? Did Guy Fawkes like the fact he was remembered every year throughout the nation as a great villain when he never actually led or committed that crime?

The weight! The weight of responsibility. Windsor Castle, the Crown Jewels, the Commonwealth. How did her ancestors feel about Tintagel and Stonehenge? She knew so much, was so full of useless information. How many people present knew that the sarsens (that is the big dolmens) weighed 45 tonnes. That's the weight of 9 elephants. Now elephants, weren't those NLF people looking for an elephant? Oh, look, they were all leaving. Maybe she would get an early night. Maybe that machine was a blessing.'

Freedom and liberty should be used properly and clearly nobody was.'

Meanwhile thousands of pamphlets were blowing in the wind.

CHAPTER THIRTY FOUR

OF ELEPHANTS, WATER LOOS AND JEWELS

The Queen's inner soliloquy continued.

'Wish it were the evening. Then I could take awff my shoes. Worst part of the job. Aching feet. Always try and slip miy shoes off under the table, but can't now. Too visible and too dangerous, given the circumstances. Oh what a moment horribilis.'

Unbeknownst to her, Nellie the elephant had packed her trunk and said goodbye to the circus.

Because it wasn't PC anymore.

Off she went with a trumpety trump, trump, trump, trump.

For every bear that ever there was

Will gather there for certain

Because today's the day the teddy bears have their picnic.

Beneath the trees they'll hide and seek

As long as they please

Cause that's the way the

Teddy Bears have their picnic.

She'll be coming round the mountain when she comes.

The little white bull.

The silly white bull,

You're a pretty little bull.

It seemed that the animals were joining in, impervious to leaflets, pounds, eggs or spit.

They're changing the guard at Buckingham Palace.

Should Gargantua stop at Trafalgar Square? No. The combustion, anyway, afforded him no choice. Stinkbomb farted forward with fantastic fortitude, landing bang in the middle of Tower Bridge. Best not to be caught unarmed, on the hop, anyway.

He was not the first to pay a visit to the Water Loo Barracks. There were signs of forced entry but the jewel house wardens had kept valiant watch.

He had a pee, the name catching him short. Not that the pee was short. Rather the reverse, causing the start of a severe flood warning.

Bless the wardens' (now rather wet) cotton socks. The job befell them to protect the jewels. And that on a small salary. Pride, honour and valour still accounted for a few. Shame they were beefeaters.

Gargantua simply stood before them. They fell to their knees before him.

'How can we defend against you, fine sir?' they asked.

'No need. I have only come to borrow your swords. Using them once every few decades hardly seems fair. I need the sword of Spiritual Justice and that of Mercy.'

'But if we give them to you, we'll get into trouble.'

'Aren't you in enough trouble already? Do I look like a crook?'

'No, but it is our job to protect. You see the Queen's not insured. We couldn't have her claim on our hands. We're good guys.'

'Would you rather not defend her against the true enemy? I might be a protector too.'

'Yes, of course, but we're just 'umble servants.'

'I thought servants had died out?'

'It's a manner of speaking, Sir, if you will. She still pays our wages, meagre as they might be.'

'And we like the costumes we wear too. It's traditional. We're here to make people laugh and take photos and have a good holiday. We're a happy team. That was, before this war erupted.'

'Now the brokers are trying to get in on the act. Did you see the break-in attempt? Bet they've got some foreign buyers interested. Last I heard it was ten to one the Koh-i-Noor would disappear. That doesn't leave much odds.'

'Is that a no?'

'Yes.'

'Then I'll have to use unorthodox methods.'

'Are you threatening us, gov?'

'Sort of. You leave me no option. Do you like travelling?'

'As it happens, I do' said Terry Diehardbelly.

'Well, if you won't betray your mistress, you'll have to come with me. Honour is a fine thing and all too rare nowadays.'

He picked them up and placed them in his mouth, just behind the teeth. That would be an adventure for them. Thankfully, Gargantua did not eat garlic.

'Sorry, but you left me no option.'

He grabbed the swords he wanted, took out the Koh-i-Noor diamond and put it in the tooth filling that had been giving him gyp.

He had better gee-up.

'Can you hear me in there? You'll still protecting her, okay? Get a load of that.'

It is said that the estimated value of that particular diamond would pay all the expenses of all the population of the entire world for half a day.

He then headed for the white tower where he borrowed King Henry's suit of armour.

CHAPTER THIRTY FIVE

OF WAKING UP, COMBS, PRICKS, DESIRE AROUSED, CHACHACHA

The sound of snoring could be heard as far afield as the Tower. Evidently, the Z Foundation was true to its words and sword. The sound of silence. The wordless words of sound. In the beginning there was sound.

Now it so happens that Zzorroa and Dartagne were on a path of self-reflection. That is to say they were the ultimate assessors of the beginning, middle and end of their journey. Only they knew what work needed to be done and only they could do it. But because they had assessed themselves clearly, this was a little more easy. If Gargantua had been able to whisk them awake, he would have done, but it was up to them. Had Bigfortydeedee and Pantagruel trained them well enough?

They might be tired and not wish to go further or they might think that they'd already arrived. But luckily, the passion to look had never ceased within them. Despite their comatose state, it was still deepening and increasing. This was in itself a sign of accomplishment.

In fact, it was in the strength of their passionate desire for truth that they mirrored each other. Their closeness could not be denied.

Well, Dartagne was on top of her. Albeit, they were so close that it caused prickles. Prickly prickles. For Dartagne, this was caused by a comb Zzorroa had tossed into her pocket, now pricking him harder by the second. Hard.

This in turn caused him to stiffen.

His own growing stubble was standing erect and pricking Zzorroa's cheeks on specific acupuncture points. Acupuncture points forbidden to be used in the normal run of things. For good cause- it tended to create gigantic pricks as well as huge arousal. Zzorroa was not used to large pricks. This was a new journey. Time for arousal for sure. As indeed for Dartagne to arise.

The pricks did their trick. The two arose. Joined and jointly.

'Oh my' he cried

'Oh oh oh Ahhh' she cried.

They were on the job within seconds. Excellent training. Got directly to the point.

'If it didn't work for you and it didn't work for me, who is the one?' Zzorroa asked.

'Mathematical probability means it must be both of us.' Dartagne replied.

'We both try?'

'Well we seemed to be joined at the hip anyway. We might as well.'

Hugging each other with one arm, they leant forward with their other and reached for the sword. Despite its length and the fact it was so hard, the hilt fell into their hand. They touched its smooth surface, sliding their hands along the blade, wondering if it would straighten to their touch. No, it seemed to like the Z shape.

'We're awake, we've arisen and we have the Z sword.'

'And what is more, neither of us is falling asleep again.'

'But does this mean we have to stick together?'

'What will happen if we take our hand off?'

'Let's try'

Dartagne felt like an immediate prick.

Zzorroa was immediately aroused.

'Stuck in the middle with you' could be heard on a cd somewhere.

'Music! The Sound of Music! We've made music!'

'I think we might be making more than that' Zzorroa added.

'We had better get out of here and on with it' Dartagne said.

'How are we going to make this work?'

'By joining. If we stay together, we can stop the war.'

'That does go against the world of today.'

'Exactly. No more independence. You can't have it your way and I can't have it my way. There is only the way.'

'That's a bit deep for me, Dartagne.'

'I thought you liked that Zzorroa.'

'Well, union and being one is a bit frightening. It's a bit intimate.'

'You prefer to remain an independent island when you have the opportunity to unite? We might lose pounds and become euros (heros in Francais, n'est ce pas?)'

'Put that way, my resistance weakens.'

'Do you know how to do the tango?'

'Better at the jerk'

'No jerking off and out would be too erratic'

'What about the can-can?'

'We could keep that for when we have to aim, otherwise it might be a bit too exhausting'

'There's always rock and roll'

'And I like it. We had definitely better use that as a method.'

'Do you think that will bring satisfaction?'

'Oh yes, for sure.'

'But let's start with a quickstep, slowstep, waltz. That should see us out of here.'

So they quickstepped, slowstepped, waltzed, rhumbaed, jived and sambaed, bossanovaed, sauntered and cha cha chaed.

They were in tune.

CHAPTER THIRTY SIX

OF UNIFORMS, GUNPOWDER, JOINING FORCES AND BALLS

A lone woman baring her breasts was camped on a tank with a soapboard which read: 'Les petits conflits font des grandes guerres'.*

Catching sight of her and agreeing, Gargantua almost tripped up over some large cannon balls which sent off a fuse in his brain. It could of course be a flash in the pan.

On the walls by the edge of the river, soldiers had assembled wearing suits of armour. They were garnitures of interchangeable pieces which could be adapted for different combat, on this occasion foot combat. The reasons for wearing them now were manifold. Firstly, it protected them.

Secondly, uniforms *always* went down well with the ladies. Many women had joined the army for the very joy of wearing a uniform. Many other women waited back home avidly watching television in the hope of catching a glimpse of their child or beloved in full regalia. It made them glow with pride.

That was indeed why the tricky problem arose. Such marvellous attire for masterful *men*. But for the ladies it was a different matter.

---

*(Little conflicts make great wars-Rabelais)

The codpiece, that is. Such a marvellous construct. Guaranteed to create immediate protection of the vital organs. Voluminous in circumference (1 metre at least and a length of no less than 80 centimetres). As the soldiers strutted forth, so too did their codpieces. With great aplomb the codpieces stopped their pride being pricked. Unlike Henry VIII's.*

But the government had singularly failed to see the error of retaining codpieces, or the need to adapt the uniform, owing to civil service cuts and general lack of communication between Sandyhearse and MODE.

Soldiers of both sexes complained that their armoured body suit made them look like Goofy. It was intended to cut spiralling casualties but some troops complained that the headgear was inelegant. Others complained that the water-cooling system regularly broke down or that the heavy suits restricted movement during combat.

Fighting for their Country was of course why they had joined but a comfortable uniform helped. Government was worried lest law suits start flying around and Mutiny break out within the ranks. A secret memorandum had been found and published before you could say 'Jack the Ripper' containing fear over the shortage of recruits and fresh enticements to be brought in: Bounty's (large coconut rations to be protected), double beds during combat, clean loos, pockets for make-up, more armoured vehicles etc, etc. But nowhere was there any mention of codpiece removal.

---

*When Henry VIII's codpiece was displayed, Victorian women who had trouble conceiving came and pricked their hairpins on the inner velvet padding to increase fertility.

The soldiers were complaining.

Having been deployed for quite a while and aware of the sticky unfolding down the river, all the soldiers were fed up with 'standing around like poofs'. (Their own terminology, not the author's). Perhaps that's probably because some of them were. There weren't any pouffes to sit on anyway. They had to really get on because it was more like being locked in a tin for months and months. Whatever side they batted on it was all the same. No space left for big girl blouses or wimps. Gone the 'don't ask, don't tell'. So *Tom Jones* started chatting to *the Deserter* about the *North West Frontier* and the *Northwest Passage*. *Mr. Lawrence* wished everyone a *Merry Christmas*, secretly terrified of the *Desert Rats* and *Zulu*. *Barry Lyndon* was keen for a *Charge of the Light Brigade* over the *White Cliffs of Dover*. But most were *Virgin Soldiers*.

Yes, it was quite hard to tell the sex of the people inside the suits but this added to the excitement. Rules had been bent.

Some soldiers were a bit bombed out anyway, and thought they were Michelin men or astronauts on the moon. Not quite recovered from the Sixties.

Putting mortar shells filled with pounds (there were enough lying about) of gunpowder in the pan which caused quite a few sparks, the soldiers discovered another major problem. There was a shortage of balls.

For it has to be said, the Army had always been unified in its concern with the one motto:

'Be the best'.

However it was quite hard to do so without balls. The few they had had deteriorated over the years and of course, some ranks didn't have any at all. How could they possibly fight without balls?

Gargantua looked around him to get the lay of the land. Around the bend in the river, more and more NLFs were crowding onto the 'I'. They seemed to be glued to it. Definitely stuck. They had started throwing their eggs at the pound employees whose money was evaporating underfoot as they carried on walking towards the enemy. Thousands were falling over on the slippery substances. Ambulances were trying to reach the formidable number of victims with broken legs but were unable to reach them.

CHAPTER 37

OF MORE BALLS, BULLETS, SOAKING WET, DANCING AND SINGING, AND THE PULVERIZING POWER OF LOVE

Gargantua diverted his irritation by playing boules and bowled the remaining balls into the river. He hadn't played for far too long and it was a welcome diversion after being cooped up in the hotel.

It was only at this point that the soldiers stopped standing around and noticed him. Any previous complaint over watery uniform issues was now richly deserved. They were soaking wet with fear. Protective suits worn against outer enemies started to suffocate them with the steam of their inner fear. They would definitely need to disarm soon. Undress or die. Come out or suffocate. Show their true colours or drown. The dripping syndrome. What had the specialist on the television said? They were definitely leaking and wished they had paid more attention.

Could somebody really exist so tall? And what was he doing with swords in his hand? The old abusers checked their rations. Maybe the gear was not so clean or green or the taps, sorry tabs, so pure? A rainbow-coloured giant. Too psychedelic for words. Was he/it for real?

At the sight of their balls quickly disappearing into the river, they knew they had to bite the bullet or they might bite the dust. They had certainly bitten off more than they could chew.

Time to use their guns. They fired bullets at Gargantua. Five hundred and thirty two thousand and sixty three bullets in one round. All at his head. To Gargantua, the bullets felt like no more than being bitten by a bug. He wanted to speak out but bit his tongue and instead, shooed them away with his hand.

Once bitten, the soldiers were definitely twice shy. Perhaps it was a result of their biting the hand that fed them. They had forgotten that the biter always gets bitten. This situation was definitely putting the bite on.

Inadvertently they had shot a single bullet at Stinkbomb. This had accidentally shot a hole in the water tank. This set off a leak which spread rapidly over the edges of the bridge and down into the Tower. Within seconds the soldiers were caught in the swell of water and were bowled out and over the tower walls. It wasn't at all Bloody.

Having so easily dispensed with the army, Gargantua headed in the direction of Big Ben. He pulled out his comb which was a hundred canes long and set with great elephants' tusks. Passing it through his hair, he brought down more than one thousand bullets. He thought they were lice and wiped his comb carefully with the flag he had taken off Buckingham Palace. Quite nice material for a handkerchief.

'If Bigfortydeedee could see me now, she would be so distressed.'

He stopped scratching and carried on his way in search of Zzorroa and Dartagne. The bullets fell like rain causing some brokers to have to take cover.

'Thousand to one, there's more where those came from'

'Thousand to two, it's going to rain bullets some more'.

Meanwhile Zzorroa and Dartagne were still joined by the sword. Dancing out of the Z Foundation, they heard the Lady of the Fountain exclaim:

'I told you so'.

The tension between them was high. They were so excited, making *the sound of music* together *dancing in the street*. The energy between them was extraordinary. It was like the feeling when you fall in love and think that feeling will last forever but multiplied by a ratio of H2O to the power of one trillion.

They had the sword. They were working in symbiosis. They could truly help Gargantua. They were so grateful to his family. Without them all, they would not be here, fulfilling their potential.

Born free. Born to be wild.

Dancing sideways along the pavements, still with jiffy bags on their feet, the sword's tip gently dragged along the ground between them. Torvill and Dean could eat their bolero. The power of their chant combined with the power of the sword had a pulverizing effect. No different from refusing to be taken off cloud nine. No different from not buying into somebody's negative view of you. No different from refusing to be brought down to earth. No different from flying high. No different from riding a kite. No different from being on top of the world. The lightness of being. They felt so very light. From the tip of the sword to the top of their heads, they tingled with joy. And they weren't even making love! They hadn't even kissed. They were transformed and transforming. They were helping the world. They were useful.

Ho hom, ho hom, and on the road we go. Ho hom ho hom ho hom ho hom. From hump to hom. Hommmmmmmmm.

Before their very sword, the leaflets disintegrated. And the more the gloss and paper disintegrated the more the sword straightened. Mission impossible possible.

The brokers had never felt so happy either. Whichever way they went there was a story. News reporters were joining the melee. To the left, unknown man and woman with the Z sword finally removed from the stone, slaying leaflets and £s in its sway. To the right, a giant heading for the House of Commons. That was seriously big news.

Water too was starting to trickle along the pavements, making the territory even more slippery. A few broke a leg on stray bullets. None wanted to give up. The stakes were too high. It was too big an adventure.

What next?

CHAPTER THIRTY EIGHT

OF STIFF WHITES, YOLKY MESSES, 8 MAJOR CONCERNS, FOGGY PEA SOUP, PUTRID SMELLS, SPRING CLEANING.

By now the Nerds for Life, the £s, the sex maniacs, the fitness fanatics, the WIs and the brokers were all stuck on or around the 'I', some in the cages, sorry, carriages, sorry pods, stuck, unable to get out or change. Others were a sticky yolky mess. Others were stiff and white. Many were broken.

If you were privy to their conversation, you would have found it impossible to distinguish between the warring factions. One thing united them in spite of the war, however much they might try to deny it. Not one thing but 72 reactions based on their major concerns. Not just about the present situation but about the past and the future.

As the 'I' spun round, the pods had tags affixed with large red lettering displaying an altogether different set of complaints. Gone the pink champagne, enter a few remaining burst balloons, and a set of demands which read as such:

1. We want pleasure
2. We want wealth
3. We want praise
4. We want to be famous

5. We don't want pain
6. We will not be losers
7. Don't blame us, it's not our fault
8. We don't want to be nobodies.

Some armoured vehicles (but not enough) and helicopters (with little if any petrol left) were standing by, but no soldiers were left to pilot them. The last had been seen bobbing along the river. The Thames had turned a putrid colour, awash with soldiers, balls, spit, broken eggs and a dash of Gargantua's pee. Yes, the Thames looked a bit like pea soup. Foggy pea soup.

All the parties considered it their right to feel the way they felt and they were all unhappy. The problem was they didn't know what would make them happy anymore and didn't have a goal. They were all sticking to their reference points. They were all sticking to their idols.

But what use was being stuck to the 'I'?

Was it useful as a whole? Was it useful in parts? Could they dismantle a carriage and put it in an attic? Could they dismantle another part and put it in a cupboard? Could they put a bit in the bin straight away? Could they put a pod in a pea?

No, most of them wanted to hang onto everything they felt or owned until after they died. Their descendants could dig it out of the ground.

The inhabitants would not give in or up.

The £s thought the WIs were all past it.

The WIs thought the Nerds needed a good hiding.

The fitness fanatics wanted to work out with the sex

maniacs.

The sex maniacs wanted to get a leg or a lot more over.

The Nerds wanted to be dominated.

The brokers were spread-eagled trying to please all.

There was just one big problem. A large round one. If one carriage got rid of another, everyone would be topsy turvy. It would be Titanic revisited. Tits up.

The WIs were keen to throw the others away like bad food out of the fridge. Some of it had such an unpleasant odour. But were they convinced? They were all partial to their own tastes and smell but they were all cheese. Mrs.Beeton, WI and master of logistic explained clearly to her pod:

'It's all about cheese. If we left the cottage cheese long enough to have the same appearance as Roquefort, no one would eat it because cottage cheese shouldn't look like that but they would eat it if they thought it was Roquefort, even if it was French.'

The Nerd Leader had never appeared, but the Nerds all held the same seemingly entrenched view that everyone should choose the Big Cheese.

Fitness fanatics were determined to avoid cheese altogether but the sex maniacs couldn't resist having a bit on the side, or titbits whenever they could get a bite.

The fact was, they were all having to get used to each other's ways because nobody wanted to rock the boat or roll the 'I' more than it was twisting already.

It was a problem. They were stuck as they were but uncomfortably sticky. They were stuck in a smelly mess and getting quite used to it which made the idea of change quite uncomfortable. If they took a link out, they would all fall down. It was quite obvious that any action from on top would affect below and any action below would affect on top. They had been so sure they wanted to win but hadn't considered the effect of getting caught up in a wheel together. It was a bit of a rat run.

The few brokers still on the loose refused to give up the gamble: it was after all, one of the greatest market studies of the mind. The one thing they couldn't gamble on was the certainty that they would be constantly happy or unhappy. They gambled on the incontrovertible fact that everything changes. They gambled on the fact *something* would affect them. That's what gave them hope, the fact they could try and control what affected them.

'Three to one, the wheel will fall'

'Two to three the glue will come unstuck'

'Five to six the top heavy carriage will fall down'

'Six to eleven, there will be serious casualties'

CHAPTER 39

OF SCIENTIFIC VIEWS, JEANS, FAITH, MONKEYS AND KNOBS

The BBC had materialised another coup. In the midst of the melee they had managed to haul in two famous scientists by the names of Shell and Dork.

Lyle Whatson conducted the interview.

'Dork, let's start with you. I had a slight problem because when I tried to find out about your work, a warning came up:

'While files on the internet can be useful, this file type can potentially harm your computer. Only install software from publishers you trust'

I found this quite worrying. Still, your work on jeans does not need much introduction so let me launch forth.

Clearing his throat:

You have always considered living after Aristotle, Newton, Darwin and Einstein a privilege. You have also said that our ancestors were bacteria, that most creatures still are bacteria and each one of our trillions of cells is a colony of bacteria. Are you now worried about the broken eggs and spit? Or are your views crumbling at the advent of a giant?'

'Has anyone actually seen the giant? Have *you* ***really*** seen him?' Dork replies.

'Of course. You can see him now if you turn to the television screen'

'*I* can't see him. I can only see what you *suggest* you have put on the screen. However it **is** an incontrovertible fact that I saw the monkeys on the way here. But then we **are** apes. Our common ancestors are the chimpanzees and gorillas. *I* would vote for the monkeys anyday. Why **not** join them? We are part of them. More important than this gargantuan nonsense.'

'But let me bring you back to the now. Now that we do have a giant in our midst. Does this mean we have a contest? Does this change your previously held strong views that you knew nothing and everyone else knew all? Whoops, did I get that wrong?'

'What I said was this: when two people meet and express opposite views, it is possible for one side to be one hundred percent wrong. Clearly, here that is you. All this nonsense about giants.

Faith is a great cop-out, the great excuse to evade the need to think and evaluate evidence. Faith is the belief in spite of, even perhaps because of, the lack of evidence'

'Other people like Soggy Posh would say that 'Doubt is intelligence gone wrong' or Pete Ackneroyd would ask: 'why is it so difficult to have faith?' 'Why do you resist so much?' Whatson continued.

'Just look at the television now'.

'I can't see the giant. Can't see him at all' Dork protested.

'But he's there on the screen in front of you.'

'But have you weighed and measured him?' Dork continued

'What is interesting about the scientific view of the world view is that it is true, inspiring, remarkable and that it unites a whole lot of phenomena under a single heading. We are all bacteria.'

'Just like the Nerds. Do you think your views could be more selfish?'

'Why because I'm wearing tight jeans? Is that so selfish? Because I know I am right?'

'Perhaps you could loosen up a bit if we bring in Morph. What about you, Morph? What do you have to say?'

'I have to say I find the whole situation wildly exciting. A giant in the world again after five hundred years. That was the last sighting, I believe. And the sound. The resonance. It's such a great repetition. What the giant is doing is very creative. Of course, we don't know where creativity comes from. Is it inspired from above? Or welling up from below? Picked up from the air? What? And then what happens is a kind of Darwinian natural selection- not every good idea survives-but each thing has a collective memory. The giant will be influenced today by the giants of the past.'

Morph is interrupted by loud snorting from Dork. Whatson cuts in:

'You mean like the story of the 100th monkey?'

'Exactly'.

Whatson adds turning to the camera:

'That's the story of the monkeys who learn a new trick on an island and within days, monkeys are performing the same trick on another island even though they haven't met or communicated...at a conscious level'.

So you believe in the Jungian approach and views on the collective unconscious applying to animals as well as human beings? '.

'It might also explain why Dork can't see the giant. Most of us have had our knobs stimulated -television knobs that is- by the vision of the giant but that doesn't prove that all the programmes on that other channel are stored inside the bit that I've stimulated, namely the tuning knob, and it could be that it's just simply part of the tuning system. I think the brain is like a tuning system and that we tune into our own memories by a process of resonance'.

'So how then, Dork, do you take to the idea that your knob hasn't been stimulated?'

'It really comes down to parsimony, economy of explanation'.

'The seventeenth century turned the world into a machine.' Morph interrupts.

'It is possible that if your knob looks like a knob, smells like a knob and performs exactly as a knob should, the sensible working hypothesis is that it is a knob' Dork contested. 'It is possible that we are just machines'.

'If we go back to the idea of nature as a living organism, the whole of nature as being alive and ourselves as living beings within a living world, a living world that has many levels of organization from molecules, atoms, cells, the whole planet, the solar system, the galaxy, the whole universe- at every level there's a kind of integrity, a wholeness that's more than the sum of the parts'.

As Morph spoke, Dork's jeans burst open, zip undone. His knob was clearly being stimulated.

'We seem to have diverted a lot from the giant. He's definitely a whole lot of parts. Do you have anything else to say about the giant?

Ah, apparently it looks as if the giant is about to speak. Now have a look for yourself. Perhaps we had better go over live to the action'.......

CHAPTER 40

OF NO TIME, BIG BEN, BUSY, JUNGLES AND ARTERIES

The time had indeed come.

Gargantua walked up and sat down in front of Big Ben.

He prepared to speak. He cleared his throat. He waited. The brokers and journalists caught up with him. Zzorroa and Dartagne glided in, sword still in hand. They sat down in front of him, having first ensured that any kind of leaflet or £ was pulverized out of sight.

'Good morning everyone' he muttered.

His voice was so gentle but carried many miles even though he spoke barely above a whisper.

'Today everyone is so very very busy. We're all living in a very busy world and everyone has to work. There is no choice but to work. Either we're busy working or we're busy looking for work. That's what we see and believe and that's what we talk about. We talk about how busy we are. To do what? Even when we're working we are busy. We are the busiest people on earth. We have no time to talk about anything else but that and that thought is like hypnotism. No time, no time, no time. We have no time to really have no time and actually we have no time to do anything. We don't even have time to think that we have the occasion to think.

We hear this background music:

'I'm so busy

I've no time'

And that is all we think about... The mantra:

'We are busy'

'We have no time'

'We are rushing'

'We are the busiest people on earth'

All of you present are hypnotised with the simple mantra:

'No time, no time, no time, no time, no time, no time, no time, no time, no time, no time'.

'Too busy, too busy, too busy, too busy, too busy, too busy, too busy'.

Big Ben chimed in the background, not the well known 'DONG' but a two-step waltz :

N O O O O O O O O O O O O O O O O O O O O O O O O

TIIIIIIIIIIIIIIIIIIIIIIIIIIIIIIIIIMe,

N O O O O O O O O O O O O O O O O O O O O O O O O

TIIIIIIIIIIIIIIIIIIIIIIIIIIIIIIIIIIIIIIIIIMe.

NOOOOOOOOOOOOOOOOOOOOOO

TIIIIIIIIIIIIIIIIIIIIIIIIIIIIIIMe.

We all hear the background music, everyone caught up in the repetitive beat.

'I'm so busy

I've no time

I'm so busy

I've no time
I'm so busy
I've no time'
Hump tilly ump tum
'I'm so busy
I've no time
I'm so busy
I've no time
I'm so busy
I've no time'

Just like a drumbeat

A chorus repeated for century upon century and increasingly so today.'

He paused.

'It's just like a jungle. That's what it looks like. From L'Undone to Antartica and back, everyone locked into a jungle of no time. Even the elephants rushing about trunks up, on strike for more time to walk across their territory, to have time to reproduce. Even the monkeys spreading leaflets at the rate of knots. Even the cows are no longer allowed to ring their bells because of 'no time to sleep factor', food being transplanted before time, to be sold 'to ripen in your own time' to customers with no time to wait for it to ripen and eat it in no time. No time to cook.

No time to go to the loo in peace. Always rushing a pee. No time to read in private on the john. Remember those days?

The Nerds and £s and brokers have spread the disease even further but the bacteria has been within us for a long time.

They are only symptoms of our general malaise. Do not judge what lies within you.

The problem is not just in l'Undone because there are 'no time' leaflets spread across the globe, millions of kilometres of 'no time' stretched across arterial roads. Arteries across the world. 'no time, no time, no time'.

It is time to change, if you will forgive the pun.'

CHAPTER FORTY ONE

OF SWORDS AND HANDS AND TIMELESSNESS

'Imagine if we lived in a world of American television, a world of reality TV. We watch these programmes and can be so offended by them and yet we act just like them. That's what I mean by 'no time'. We enter into the game so much and yet think we're so above it all. That is specifically what we need to cleanse.

When we go around believing in triple and quadruple reality television, we go around thinking the world is so very unappealing, polluted and stupid. *That* person who judges it, that is what we want to eradicate.'

So saying, to a stunned audience, Gargantua swished his rainbow cloak around him and stood up. Reaching up, he carefully dismantled Big Ben's hands and laid them on the grass in front of him...Zorroa and Dartagne scooped them up with their free hand.

He then walked across the bridge to the 'I'. Without hesitation, he picked it up and dipped it in the Thames, shaking it all about and spinning the pods round as he did so. The sensation for the inhabitants was not dissimilar

to a salad being washed in your favourite wedding present gift, a salad spinner,

or a washing machine spinning around multicoloured clothes when you had forgotten your child's dinky toy car was in your dressing gown pocket

or that the piece of chewing gum was stuck to your child's sock

or the boiled sweet stuck to the condom packet in the teenager's handkerchief.

Or the shredded torn paper tissue statically stuck to the slightly damp duvet cover with the still wet sheet caught up inside.

Or a car when you change gear at the wrong moment or brake too late going over speedhumps. Clonk, clonk, clonk. Clonkety clonk.

Or an aeroplane when going through storm und drang.

Or your stomach when you've drunk three cups of tea, four pints of beer, eaten fried eggs and chips with ketchup and a packet of chocolate digestives.

Most of the brokers, WIs, £s employees and NLF members fell off or out of the pods into the river, joining the mass of soldiers, balls and pea soup but a few remained, stuck to their seats. He raised the wheel again and blew on it.

Now you just might remember that as a child Gargantua had a football pitch in his bedroom. He hadn't played for a long while but the urge overcame him at such a good opportunity. The balls had been good for boules, but the 'I' was much larger and easier to kick.

Lifting it onto his foot, he gently plopped it up into the air, aiming it perfectly to land 13 miles away where it rolled directly underneath the Arch of the new Wembley Stadium, much like a roulette ball slopping into the right hole.

The particularly stubborn eight aggregates remaining in the 'I' fell onto the pitch. They lay dazed, wet, befuddled, confused, angry, despairing, dotty, petrified, enraged, stupefied, mummified, obtuse, crooked, deviant, off centre, out of orbit, rambling, aberrant, roving, loose, footloose, random, erratic, off-beam, lost, stray, astray, misdirected, misaimed, off target, off the mark, off the fairway, in the rough, twisted, zigzagging and crooked.

The new Wembley Stadium was built to the highest specifications, intended to be the most spectacular stadium in the world. Internationally renowned architects had ensured that the state-of-the-art facilities were matched by a design that created an electric atmosphere, making it the ultimate stage for major events. Perhaps they had not quite imagined such a major event.

Amateur DVD cameras had footage. Journalists and television crews rushed to Wembley as fast as possible. The attraction was magnetic. The atmosphere definitely charged. The setting large.

The arch alone could let the Channel Tunnel train run through it. The pencil ends of the Arch were 18 million times as heavy as an average pencil. Gargantua, a little thirsty drank from the 500 steel straws, each large enough to hold over 850 pints of milk and attached to giant 70 ton hinges.

The collective length of the cables used to lift the Arch into place would stretch from the centre of London to the White Cliffs of Dover (130kms). The amount of paint needed to coat the Arch was enough to cover the ceiling of the Cistine chapel more than 19 times.

Gargantua leaned on it. Luckily it could handle his strength weighing in at a mighty 1750 tonnes, the equivalent of 275 double decker buses or ten Jumbo Jets.

People started to drive their cars again with flags hanging out of every orifice. Crowds amassed (nothing to do with you loving) in record time, desperate to see divine retribution. No peace for the wicked, no mercy for the enemy. Time to slaughter the victim. Time to win. Time to ......they were at it already.....they had forgotten Gargantua's dictum...they were trying to make time out of time.

Some travelled at the speed of light. Others at a snail's pace. Some from outremer, some from just down the road, all heading for the magnetic attraction of a match.

Clomp, clomp, clomp.

Clomp, clomp, clomp.

Pitter patter, pitter patter

Clippety clop, clippety clop.

The wheels on the bus go round and round, round and round....

Brrrrrrrrr.Brrrrrrrr.Brrrrrr.

CHAPTER FORTY TWO

OF TRANSFORMATION, TAKING THE PLUNGE, DAMS AND DYKES

He picked up the now-completely empty 'I' and put it back in the Thames. It bobbed along with the other polluted pea pods.

Television cameras were still trying to film it all but everyone was out of time and could only take pictures of individual takes rather than the over-all panorama. It all seemed to be happening so quickly. Dartagne and Zzorroa were speeding around L'Undone on the strength of love, pulverizing any remaining leaflets in their stride. Three swords on the go made an easy job of it.

For through what some might refer to as alchemy, Big Ben's hands had been transformed into the Sword of Justice and the Sword of Mercy. Nobody had seen Gargantua remove the swords he had extracted from the Tower. Perhaps he was a magician as well. Perhaps it was alchemy. It was all a bit vague. Some people still saw Big Ben's hands.

Previous government warnings were being ignored as people rushed out, heading for the Stadium. The power of attraction and compulsion was too strong to avoid. Now the streets were safe and the enemy defeated, they wanted to crow over the victors.

Thanks to John Travole privately piloting his Gulliver Express Bling 707, images from l'Undone were finally broadcast across the globe.

'TIME HAS STOPPED IN L'UNDONE. AFTER WAR ERUPTING BETWEEN NERDS AND POUNDS, THE L'UNDONE 'I' HAS BEEN WASHED, KICKED, TRANSPLANTED AND DUMPED IN THE RIVER BY A GIANT. YES, A GIANT. YES, YOU DID HEAR CORRECTLY, A GIANT. A GIANT HAS APPEARED OUT OF NOWHERE AND IS TRANSFORMING THE WORLD AS WE KNEW IT. HE SINGLEHANDEDLY TOOK OFF THE HANDS OF BIG BEN. HE SOAKED THE L'UNDONE 'I' IN THE THAMES BEFORE KICKING IT INTO WEMBLEY STADIUM.

HE THEN SHOOK OUT THE STICKY INHABITANTS WHO ARE NOW WANDERING DAZED AROUND THE PLAYING FIELD, AND DUMPED THE 'I' BACK IN THE RIVER THAMES.

AS IF THIS WEREN'T ENOUGH NEWS, OVER TO THE RIGHT YOU WILL CATCH SIGHT OF THE OTHER EXTRAORDINARY HEROES OF THE DAY. A LADY AND MAN, OF UNKNOWN ORIGIN, HAVE SINGLEHANDEDLY PULLED OUT THE Z SWORD (WHICH APPEARS TO HAVE STRAIGHTENED) AND ARE NOW PULVERIZING ALL TREACHEROUS LEAFLETS AND POUNDS FOUND ON THE PAVEMENTS WITH WHAT APPEARS TO BE BIG BEN'S HANDS (OR IS IT TWO OTHER SWORDS?) . THAT WOULD DEPEND ON YOUR VISION.

THERE IS ONE MAJOR CONCERN, HOWEVER, AND THAT IS THE THAMES. THE THAMES IS SWELLING AS A RESULT OF THE AMOUNT OF POLLUTION AND JUNK THAT HAS BEEN DUMPED IN IT.

WHAT WITH BALLS,

BOBBING SOLDIERS,
INNUMERABLE POUND EMPLOYEES,
COUNTLESS NERDS,
THE LONDON 'I' CONSTRUCTION,
EGGS AND
SPIT
THERE SEEMS TO BE NO LIMIT TO THE DUMPING.

REMARKABLY, THERE HAVE BEEN NO DEATHS IN THIS WAR. ONLY BROKEN LEGS. SIXTY SIX BROKEN LEGS. THE GERMAN GOVERNMENT HAS SENT THE PRIME MINISTER A MESSAGE TO ASSURE HIM THAT THIS CAN BE BUT GOOD LUCK.

AND NOW, PEOPLE ARE COMING OUT OF PURDAH AND HEADING EN MASSE FOR WEMBLEY.'

Back in the studio (*the author does apologize for this 'back to the studio' repetition but we do live in the modern world where television rules and it might still be infinitely preferable to the old Aeneid Virgilian tracts or detailed Tolstoyan Napoleonic war descriptions*) so back in the studio, a variety of experts were putting their viewpoint out of time forward:

'There was last night the greatest tide that ever was remembered in England to have been in this River all Whitehall having been drowned' Samuel Pepys spoke on 7th December 1663.

John Stow from 'The Chronicles' in 1236 reported:

'The river is overflowing and in the great Palace of Westminster men did row with worried wherries in the midst of the hall.'

The Times recorded that 14 people drowned in 1928 and a further 300 in 1953.

Watery Limb from the Environment Agency 19994 commented:

'The Thames Barrier is now being raised. With the dangerously high tidal surge threat, the rising sector gates are being moved up about 90% from their riverbed position and the four radial gates are being bought down into the closed defence position. The gates thus form a continuous steel wall facing down the river ready to stem the tide.'

And Ken Tsi from the 'Advance research into the effects of water on the mind' added:

'It all comes from the river of our mind, of our emotions. If I were a practising engineer and hadn't yet built a big dam, I would just have to do studies on the strength of both the river and river bed and check whether they were solid or not. The cement, the walls have really got to be as strong as the river's current and be in proportion.

So even if it takes ages, if I don't want flooding, the only option is building a dam high up enough or putting in dykes.

Dykes are more cosmetic but stopping the river at the source is the only solution that really gets at the cause of it.

So first I have to do cosmetic mind training and then the only thing that can free me is when I realise that my emotions, their emotions, your emotions, all emotions have no reality.

I do definitely have to build dykes, so that while I'm trying to apply the final solution, it is not disturbed by the outpouring of water, outpouring of the river flooding me all the time'.

Student dripping wet, recently recouped from the river:

'But what about if the dams or dykes aren't strong enough? I keep on building dams and dykes and I keep getting flooded. And then I go and build my camp elsewhere but that doesn't feel right because I'm leaving my family behind and it just goes round and round in circles. '

'Maybe you should do some study of that river. A survey of the river and what kind of material you need to use to build those dykes and eventually to build the dam on it.

Imagine this river were to overflow every time it rains and you were to complain to the council every time. They would just say:

'oh yes, we've studied those issues and we've contracted contractors to sort it out' but then nothing happens. And then of course, the next time it actually floods thousands of peoples' homes. Then they will do something. So actually, with this river there is the possibility of working before, during and after. And most often we cannot work before and find it impossible to work during but there's definitely no excuse not to work afterwards. We do have to clean up then. As far as that clean up is concerned, we should apply the attitude of purification.'

'All I know is balls and dykes don't mix well together and there's rather a lot of balls floating around' the weather forecaster interrupted.

CHAPTER FORTY THREE

OF THE HEART

Of course, so much depended on the heart of things.

A conglomerate of keen reporters reached the Couple of the Day, Zzorroa and Dartagne. They formed a band in front of them and encircled them as they jiffied along, magnificent swords in hand.

'Please tell us who you are. The world wants to know. How have you managed to defeat the leaflets and pounds? How have you managed to withdraw the sword? How can you jiffy around so quickly? How can you *do* all this?'

'Zzorroa with the extra Z, born to serve Queen and Country but most of all, Gargantua. At your service' Zzorroa spoke, shocked by her own self-assurance. Where had her old timid self gone? She felt no fear whatsoever but the complete faith that what she was doing and saying was good.

'Dartagne, born to seek truth at all cost and to defeat falsehood and protect mankind, Gargantua's servant at your service'. Dartagne bowed to them.

'No idea how we managed to do it. Do know we couldn't do it alone. We are the one. As you all are. Diddle diddle diddle dum...' Zzorroa continued:

'He couldn't raise it without me and I couldn't get aroused without him and we couldn't stay awake without the sword.

Once we realized we needed to act together, it all flowed smoothly. One thing can never live independently of another.'

'Wow!'

It's all to do with the heart.

'According to the Hippocratics, the heart is the basis of life and all activities take place in the heart. Aristotle assumed we were in our hearts. Galen that our Venus was a tidal river back and forth to the heart. Alberti that our emotions, heart and health were linked under the humoral system. Abisena swore the heart was at the centre of the body. In the Renaissance, courtiers like Sir Philip Sydney operated behind a mask and the heart was hidden behind the mask and gave a psychological identity to the inside of the organ. Shakespeare advocated that the heart was a metaphor for thinking and being. Francis Bacon cannibalised the heart. Only in the 19th century was the heart separated from the body, brain and soul. Descartes made the pumping of the heart all important, an organ that could be maintained without a soul. Hobbs turned the heart into a spring. Medical therapy got out of touch with the advances of the body.' Dartagne long-windedly continued.

But now!' Zzorroa interrupted

'The heart is where we feel things rather than think things. Romantics see into the heart of things. No more heartbreak hotels, it will now be heart warming to follow your heart instead of eating your heart out. From our own experience we can tell you that heart to heart is the best way to dance. Access to the heart leads to all sorts of transmutations. If you have your heart in the right place rather that your heart in your mouth, you can achieve your heart's desire and can wear your heart on your sleeve by knowing the truth in your heart of hearts. So with a change of heart, you can

heartmake rather than heartbreak.' Zzorroa soliloquised.

'Trust in your heart but when men are at war with one another, the Soul of the World can hear the screams of battle.' Paulo the alchemist chipped in.

'Why do we have to listen to our hearts? The boy asked

'Because, wherever your heart is, that is where you'll find your treasure.' Paulo replied.

'But my heart is agitated, it has its dreams, it gets emotional and it's become passionate.' The boy continued

'Well, that's good. Your heart is alive. Keep listening to what it has to say.' Paulo retorted.

'For goodness sake, a heart is a hollow muscular organ that pumps blood through the circulatory system by rhythmic contraction and dilation' Dork appeared out of nowhere and contested, jeans falling down his legs.

'No, no, it's all to do with resonance. We can hear the sound of your sword swishing and it makes us feel alive. It's stirring some old memory and we're waking up. We're standing up. We can hear the truth.' Enthusiastic young teenagers enjoined.

'We're with you, Zzorroa and Dartagne. We're with you.'

Zzorroa and Dartagne swished in front of the teenagers' hearts with the sword, forming the letter Z. The effect was immediate. The kids were grinning from ear to ear even more.

'Thanks. That's cool. We're even more awake now. Better than nerd life anyday.'

'What complete and utter nonsense. Let's put an end to it.'

Dork yelled walking up to them and making a grab for the sword.

Instinctively Zzorroa and Dartagne protected themselves and swished a Z to the front of Dork's heart as well.

The effect was immediate. He coughed and spluttered and for a brief second felt nothing but empty, part of the whole, perceived deep luminosity, creating a sense of pure orgasmic delight. A state with which he was not very familiar.

He blinked 500 times in rapid succession, his trousers shot back up and did themselves up of their own accord and he remained speechless. Another first.

'Delusion born from ignorance is the worst disaster-bearing demon. No ordinary enemy however cruel can harm you beyond this lifetime. But the emotions are more formidable enemies and have harmed you since time immemorial. They never stop encouraging you to act wrongly and consequently cause you great suffering. We are brandishing the sword of transcendent knowledge and annihilating the demon of attachment to 'I' and the reality of phenomena'. Dartagne spoke clearly and lucidly.

'Compassion needs no proof from science though it will come. It is there for anyone to experience. Parents' love for their children or any other form of altruism is 'evidence' for the existence of compassion....Some have had their brains tested to see the difference in brain activity but that has only concerned neuroplasticity rather than compassion itself. Compassion is the beginning as well as its substance and its result.'

CHAPTER FORTY FOUR

OF WATER PURIFICATION, TAKING THE PLUNGE, AND SHAKE IT ALL ABOUT

Gargantua had not finished his mission. He was in his element.

Now, you might have forgotten that the Tower Guards had been placed in his mouth. They were having a bit of a struggle. Gargantua overcome with thirst had drunk the milk from the Stadium, causing his mouth to gush. The guards had been sitting on the shred of lettuce leaf that was caught between his teeth: the lettuce leaf being a frisee rather than the ready-mixed coz or new fad tangy rocket variety. He would have done anything for a home grown bio-dynamic organic version but had not had the opportunity to visit the farmer's market.

En route to the river, he had found a 24 hour '*we never stop working and so charge you an arm and a leg*' supermarket and had availed himself of KP peanuts, cashews, raisins, and unable to resists temptation, 4567 bags of salt and vinegar, cheese and onion, plain salted crisps, Pringles and kettles and hadn't been able to resist a further 3982 litres of Diet Coke.

The poor guards were overcome, struggling to shelter themselves from the danger of an inundation under the banks of his teeth. The flood of coke almost carried them away into the gulf of his stomach. But one of them by chance, groping with his stick, struck hard against the cleft of a hollow tooth and hit the mandibulary sinew or nerve of the jaw, which put Gargantua to very great pain. To ease himself therefore of his smarting ache, he reached for the bark of the Norwegian pine tree set up in Trafalgar Square and picked his teeth with the trunk.

The trunk edged the Koh-i-Noor diamond out of his mouth as he spat it into his hand. The guards tumbled out at the same time, feeling they had been on the most extraordinary adventure known to man. Poseidon. Helter skelter, the big wheel, the Sizzler, Twist, Nemesis, Nimrod, Noah's Ark, Xtreme, eliminator, Storm, Booster, flying coaster, reverse bungee, rollercoaster and Waltzer in one fair swoop.

For the few remaining Latinists in the world today, it was explained as such:

'Quum irasceretur furor eorum in nos, forsitan aqua absorbuisset nos. Torrentem pertransivit anima nostra' signifying: 'When he drank the great draught, when the stream of his water carried us to the thicket'...For the informed among you, you will pick up on the reference to prophecy.

Overcome again, with the need to pee, Gargantua did do so in such copious measure that the liquid took away the feet of stray pedestrians and caused the fountain to burst its banks as well. The lady of the Fountain was furious, appearing specifically to tell him:

'I am on your side. No need for that'

Gargantua retorted:

'Do not doubt, dear Lady, I know that of course. Do you not know that positive thinking will strengthen your immune system? You, of all people, know that immunity is love.'

The Lady of the Fountain replied:

'Ah ha. I hadn't realized you were aware of Ma Emotionato's work on heating water in a microwave. Very interesting. He showed that when using distilled water, crystals were deformed and incomplete. Using water shown the words 'love and gratitude' the water formed complete crystals. In other words, love and gratitude were able to make the water immune to the damaging effects of the magnetic field. Combine the words 'love and gratitude' and you have water crystals with a diamond-like brilliance'.

'You are the one' The Lady of the fountain repeated and as if a needle were stuck on an old LP, she continued to say

'You are the one'

'You are the one'

to every passer-by.

Gargantua walked on and stood in the middle of Waterloo Bridge. It *would* have to be.

The water beneath him did indeed appear turbulent and menacing. L'Undone was in even greater danger than before. People who had bought expensive flats by Cheyne Walk or Chelsea Embankment or further along by the Tower on the up and coming regeneration quickbuck canary scheme were worried sick. Why was the Barrier not strong enough? Why had the estate agents not warned them? Were they covered by insurance? What was the small print about war and natural disasters? Why had they been too busy to read the small print? Same with every contract- always check the small print. Too late now!

The animals had been cleverer and all had scarpered to

drier zones. Church bells started to ring- that is the churches still in existence- or those who still had bell-ringers to pull the cords- or those which hadn't been sold to private owners- or those that weren't just putting on musical concerts- or those that weren't locked up. Yes, many had to scrabble to find someone with a key who could open up their treasures. The Notre Dame Churches still did the best. Funny that, must be the resonance. Followed by St.Paul's, only coming in second because the bell-ringers tripped up over a rather long silk trail.

So as a symphony or cacophony, again, depending on your perception, played around Town, Gargantua stood in silence, cupping the famous diamond in his hand and thereby causing the guards to squeeze out of his palm with huge difficulty and hang onto the fine strands of hair on his fingers.

Gargantua stood and then sat, feet dangling over the edge of the bridge walls. He breathed in

Fhhhhhhhhhhhhhhhhhhhhhhhhhhhhhhhhhhhhhhhhhhhhhhhhhh-hhhht

And breathed out

SHhhhhhhhhhhhhhhhhhhhhhhhhhhhhhhhhhhhhhhhhhhhhhhhhh-hh

Please refer to chapter 5 if you have forgotten his method.

He thought of his father, he thought of his mother, he thought of their enduring and unadulterated love for him. He thought how hard they had travailed to help him and guide him to a healthy life. He thought how wonderful it was to be alive, how just this moment of consciousness was so very precious. He admired the amazing quality of conscious experience, regardless of its actual content. He thought of his teachers and how he would not be where he was without them. He thought of his enemy and realized without even them, he would not have reached the point he was at.

He cleared his mind until there was but love and awareness. Love, awareness, gratitude. Love, awareness, gratitude.

The Koh-i-Noor shone with a brilliance never seen before.

A single tear emanated from his right eye.

He saw a lone lotus flower passing by. He bent down and placed the diamond on the lotus leaf.

In that very instant all of the negativity in the Thames was dissolved and transformed. Within seconds the river turbulence subsided and people managed to climb out unimpeded, bright smiles on their faces. The water itself took on the lustre of diamonds, diamond crystals in each and every particle of water reaching boundlessly into the greater ocean.

CHAPTER FORTY FIVE

OF SLAVES, INEVITABLE DUE DATE, JUDGE DREAD, FOOTBALL AND ROYALTY

The stadium was full to bursting. Touts were making a roaring trade. People were full of happiness. The war was over. A few stubborn 'idiots' soon to be vanquished. The masses came to gloat and get satisfaction from watching the enemy suffer. They brought banners and whistles and good cheer.

Not a campervan was left for hire in the whole of Europe. Recreational vehicles were seen ferrying fans up and down the motorway so they could marinate themselves in the real atmosphere of the international festival of football.

The sticky remaining Nerds, brokers, WIs, £s and 'I'addicts had taken refuge in the changing rooms where the ground curators had locked them in.

It so happened that the English football team had a match planned for that very day. It had all been touch and go as to whether they would perform but, with the advent of Gargantua, and the clear-out by Zzorroa and Dartagne, the okay was given. Not that the English team was entirely English or totally oriented to the foot. It comprised the greatest members ever assembled:

Merdonna, a hulking proposition, in disco garb

Beckandcall, Roman toga with gold belt

G. Breast, two hip flasks jutting out of pockets

Navre Itsover, bionic extra arm with tennis ball in biceps

Peely, in perambulator having problems getting it up

W. Tiger, of superb technique, putting along juggling golf balls

J. mc In (yet another) row, wielding racket and yelling

On the other side of the world, Sherlock Columbo, a specialist researcher, previously based in Hawaii Five O, had gone out of his way to investigate the whereabouts of the Nerds' teacher. The leader had last been seen paying a visit to a psychic who had told him that he would die the following morning at midday when something would fall on his head and kill him.

The Leader naturally refused to believe that, as indeed he refused to believe any higher authority than himself, as indeed he regretted consulting anyone on the subject anyway. 'I am 956 years old anyway so I know best.' He fumed out and hired a helicopter that dropped him off in the middle of a remote desert, unvisited as yet by 4x4's. 'I will show them' he thought and sat chuckling in the eleven a.m. heat. At 11.59.59 seconds, just before Big Ben's hands were removed, a vulture flew over and dropped a rock straight onto the leader's head. Plop. Life over.

It is said his last words were: 'I should have listened to my teacher. I should not have thought I knew it all. Next time....' But that could have been just rumour. The moral to be drawn was that when your time is up, your time is up. Due date is due date. The other moral is to always have good counsel-someone live and someone wise, able to beat the shit out of you when you go wrong.

Happiness and suffering are produced when actions are combined with necessary conditions.

Brian Johnson, just returned from 'latest research in outer space' made an apparition, mike in hand.

Judge Dread, High Court Judge who took silk in 2121 as Crown Chancery held the coveted position as referee. Wearing white wig, red knee length rugby socks, black trainers, bright orange nylon polo shirt, black and white polka dot boxer shorts Scottish silk kilt, Nepalese leather whip and whistle tied around his neck, he truly looked the part.

National and international consciousnesses were present. People were interacting. For indeed, football is a potent force. It had been known to bring down governments, incite wars and create moments of international harmony.

The prisoners were brought into the arena, looking most dishevelled and confused. The crowd roared and chanted.

'Down with Nerds'

'Down with Nerds'

'We want BeckandCall.

'We want BeckandCall'

'Rule Britannia'

'Merdonna, Merdonna'

A giant screen showed pictures of Merdonna roaring around on a Triumph Bonneville.

'You are the champions. We are the champions' they chanted, Mexican wave after Mexican wave.

The prisoners were desperate to make a great escape but there was no hope left. Ball boys, specially trained on a ten year course to catch the ball in a foolproof way, garnered the circumference.

All eyes were drawn away for a few moments as the young Prince arrived. He took one look at the prisoners and ordered:

'Let them eat Duchy Original cake, let them all eat Duchy Original Cake'

Prisoner Nr 1, Mrs Beeton, caught a slice on her umbrella tip.

'Not bad, prefer MarksExpensive's. Wouldn't give it first prize'

Prisoner Nr 2, Uriah Heap, was pelted and found it stuck to the egg yolk in which he was already dripping

Prisoner Nr 3, Jean Valjean, tried to give it to the other victims

Prisoner Nr 4, Marquis Saddo, presented his backside and got a hiding

Prisoner Nr 5, Metall G. Bill, wasn't hungry anymore

Prisoner Nr 6, Rambo Schwarz, stuffed as many as he could catch down his throat

Prisoner Nr 7, Ma O. Marks missed the food whilst still trying to hand out leaflets still tucked into his socks.

CHAPTER 46

OF FOOTBALL, VARYING SIZE BALLS, THRUSTS AND RUNS

The prisoners didn't know what had hit them. They were trying to work out how they had ended up in an arena. Seeing a lion with an Aslan Tshirt in the audience made them nervous. A few red bulls with cylindrical tin bodies were wobbling their heads. Rather a lot of them, making the audience even more hyper. Not to mention the odd egg. The place was ripe for salmonella poisoning. The blood lust of the spectators, populus and emperors alike disturbed the prisoners' modern sensibilities.

'Ave imperator, morituri te salutant'

Almost 40 000 fans had faced the sweltering heat and risk to paint the town red and white. Back home, pubs and front rooms heaved with tens of millions.

Noone wanted to miss the party.

It was now that the prisoners huddled *together* in the hope of defending themselves, differences forgotten. How to quell the threat?

Everyone was salivating.

'L'Undone, l'Undone, l'Undone'

Confusion still reigned.

The knock came for the football team to leave the dressing-room and face the prisoners. They were all pumped up and ready to rumble, bubbly and confident.

The whistle went off.

Merdonna came running in from the blind side to nick the ball away from Mrs. Beeton's feet. A great skill to acquire, a sneaky interception requiring good timing that was as infuriating for midfielders as it was profitable for opponents, disrupting a side's rhythm before they had got going. Add to that that Mrs Beeton didn't know what she was playing or meant to be doing. She had no more idea about football than a poodle about flights to Mars. She was still pondering the relative qualities of the Duchy biscuit when Merdonna's hand seemed to push his ball in.

'It was the hand of God' he was to allege.

Hand or no hand, Mrs. Beeton retaliated with a brolly up his backside.

Whistles went mad. Red cards everywhere. The bulls reared their heads.

Both were carted off. She od'd on too much excitement whilst his wandering hand led to the last ever illegal excuse before successful rehab. He was later to quote 'the miracle brolly effect'. 'It was the best shot ever'.

The audience was ready for excitement, tantrums, diving controversies, a regular drugs bust and an incident or two between rival fans. The beauty and the beast were on show.

Earlier in the week, Breast had promised to get physical with Rambo, to try and rough him up in the firm belief that officials would allow more contact with a big man. Conceding 900 inches to his adversary, he could hardly expect to compete properly in the air.

The coach had expanded the repertoire, opponents thus unable to say for sure what was coming next.

Interviewed before the game he had explained:

'If we win, then it will leave us feeling calm. Otherwise we'll have to redouble our efforts. But to tell the truth, we're thinking of nothing other than a win.'

Brian Johnston was loving it:

'Both BBC and ITV are broadcasting simultaneously so that the phoney war that people usually expect of them is not actually correct. The war is over, now is just a game. Let us remember Bobby Moore's immortal words:

'We were more than a team. We were a formidable nation, bonded and held together by our will to win for England'

The battering ram power of Tiger trying to break down Saddo on defence had made Ma. O. Marks desperately fight the fires ignited by the incendiary forward line of Itsover and Inyetanotherrow.

Looks like both sides were undergoing a metaphoric heart transplant and indulging in a little surgical/moral renewal and testing if they have the right winning formula.

They're into all-round commitment and team spirit.

After a shaky start in which they struggled to gain possession, they were all acquitting themselves magnificently.

We have not had scenes like this for forty years. These are young men, very talented but who have had to take on a huge responsibility. The only difference is that they were already very very wealthy. Winning will not make them financially but it will make them as men.

The big guns might be under threat from the wounded animals. There is fortitude among the flair. The enduring determination of the team to see off opposing factions remains as strong as their hunger to withstand the gathering challenge for their place. They lust for victory and glory with efficiency, sweat and talent.'

England had its usual star-filled squad but it was the Prisoners who showed the wild-card, Uriah Heap, dribbling and passing as if he could light up the team for years to come.

The defence was robust. The talismanic striker, Tiger, only recently returned from a broken leg had his pressure cranked up.

They were all trying to avoid an early plane ride home.

England, the undoubted favourites were staggered by the organized and increasingly savvy and difficult to break down opponents.

The England defender, Peely, was held back as the striker, Ma O Marks pulled his dreadlocks. It was a serious offence and committed just in the referee's view so he had to be punished. The referee, only too familiar with hair pulling pain, ruled there was a foul and allowed the goal to stand.

England needed to raise the quality of its game. It was crucial to give themselves a breathing space before the knockout stages.

Performance was becoming a pressing issue. It was all because they had used too many long balls too early in the game. They hadn't got enough thrust.

CHAPTER FORTY SEVEN

OF GIANT STRIDES, LIGHT AND AWARENESS

What England needed to win was a forward thrust from Itsover. She (whoops, nobody was meant to know) thrust herself with all the vigour of determination, with a corker of a smash of superlative panache and style.

The speed and skill of both sides provided a memorable spectacle for the worldwide television audience. They were all making giant strides. **No, that would be later.** The whole tournament had been lit up by some mesmerising football, on a different plane from any previously seen.

Whose thrust would make for the next score? Who could not do without?

But dark clouds had been gathering and suddenly covered the entire stadium. At an irritating one all, the clouds bore down with such strength that even the floodlights failed as darkness fell. The players fell to the ground as well, unable to see a thing. They wandered around like headless chickens or lost sheep or blind man's buff or murderers in the dark or crazed rabbits or men in a duel or Russian rouletters.

The audience roared even louder. Viewers around the globe hit the back of their tellies. Still pitch black.

Zzorroa and Dartagne arrived milli-seconds later, swords

still in hand, non-plussed by the lack of light.

Audience, prisoners and players behaved alike, displaying self-importance. All were open targets for the painful arrows of anger, obsession, pride and jealousy. They were all afraid of renouncing and depriving themselves of the win-lose faculty.

Jean Valjean was the only miserable wretch with presence of mind. He yelled as loudly as he could:

'Would you like the clouds to clear? Would you like the light to shine? Would you like some clarity? Would you like to touch the sky?'

The crowd yelled in unison:

'Yeeeeeeeeeeeeeeeeeeaaaaaaaaaaaaaaaaaaaaaaaaaaaaa aaaaaaaaaaaaahhhhhhhhhhhh'

'Then you've got to apply the appropriate medicine'

'Boooooooooooooooooooooooooooooohhhhhhhhhhhh-hhhhhhhhhhhhhhhhhh' went the audience.

'Do you want a win-win situation? It's your choice.' He pressed on.

'Boooooooooooooooooooooooooooooohhhhhhhhhhhh-hhhhhhhhhhhhhhhhhh'

went the audience, starting to throw empty cans on the pitch. For, yes, many were quite inebriated.

'Money won't work' Metall G Bill admitted.

'And gloss fades to nothing' Itsover conceded.

There were those amid the audience who thought a draw would satisfy both their requirements. The conspiracy theory. Would any believe that the team who marched behind the cross of St George would consider cooking up a result with an enemy? Honours even, both progress? Or annihilation?

The brokers still resisted, wanting to go for broke.

No, here was a chance to light a fire in the darkness.

Dartagne and Zzorroa stood up.

'Have you not had enough? All this war for nothing and now retribution has led only to darkness. What is the point in that? You've all been attached to someone and enslaved by some experience or other just like the prisoners and team in front of you. But they are only reflections. That power fades, as easily as the pictures vanish when the television channel is changed. Anyone here who has not been prey to the prisoners' foibles can come and fight me- eh- us.' Dartagne spoke, even he, still unused to 'the one'.

The crowd shut up, well aware of the sword's power.

'Look at the two of us. We are the one. You are the one. There is only one team. I couldn't do it alone. He couldn't do it alone. We had to join. Want to get the light back?' Zzorroa asked.

'Yeeeeeeeeeeeeeeeeeeeeeeeeeaaaaaaaaaaaaaaaaaaa ahhhhhhhhhhhhhh' the crowds roared.

'I didn't hear that. Could you shout that out a bit louder?' she asked again.

'Yeeeeeeeeeeeeeeeeeeeeeeeeaaaaaaaaaaaaaaaaaaa aahhhhhhhhhhh'

'Then believe it. Believe you can touch the sky. Wake up to find out that you are the eyes of the world, Wake now, discover that you are the song'.

'Be the dance of awareness.

Get up, stand up

Stand up

For the light
Hold hands, cold hands
Make for a warm heart.'

A few hesitated, of course. Far too palsywalsy. Far too unBritish. Far too drunk. Far too intimate. Far too risky. Far too energetic. Far too way out.

'So you want to stay in the dark? You're not prepared to give it a try? The other way was definitely not working...' Dartagne said, waving the Z sword about.

Finally even the most recalcitrant conceded. The rhythm was too much to resist. They all stood up and joined. Each and everyone. And as they did, so too did the cloud evaporate.

And the light did shine once again.

The audience went wilder than any audience ever recorded in history. They cheered so very much that volumes on tellies had to be turned down to the lowest level. Clapometers broke.

Power to the people. Power to the one.

They knew it was **they** who had done it. They knew it had been up to them.

Who cared about annihilation when they had made light work?

They cheered more and more and more.

Even the ref didn't want to stop. He was one of them for once.

They were no longer miserable. And there was more to come.

Ooo yeeeaaahhh.

CHAPTER 48

OF NEWSPAPER HEADLINES AND GARGANTUA'S WORDS

As the cloud dispersed, Gargantua, Koh-i-Noor diamond in hand, became visible, sitting cross-legged in the centre of the stadium. It was hard to make him out for the light.

He breathed in and he breathed out.

He breathed in and he breathed out.

One two, one two, one two.

Zzorroa and Dartagne shooshed everyone with their swords over their mouths and sat down in front of him.

The spectators followed suit. After all, this giant had stopped the war. This giant had transformed the enemy. This giant had purified the river and stopped the flood. And now, this amazing giant was sitting before them.

What could they do but sit with him? Even the Prince thought his biscuits weren't quite up to Gargantua. Even the Prince sat in the monstrous carbuncle, awed by the light.

Gargantua sat.

And carried on sitting.

And everyone sat.

And carried on sitting.

Everyone breathed in and breathed out.

We don't know for exactly how long because we were still

out of time. But the audience did hear. This is what they heard:

....

....

....

....

....

THE NEWS

Momentous Wembley football match was overcome with black clouds.

Heroes, Zzorroa and Dartagne, with every single person joining, made light work. The l'Undone Giant, Gargantua sat before all.
He breathed in and he breathed out and said:

INSIDE: OPINION 10 • PETER TORY 11 • SPORT 39-58 • STARS & CROSSWORDS 90 • WEATHER 94

....

....

The following morning, whenever that was, for the first time in history, all newspaper front pages were identical, universally printing the same thing across the globe
in all 1022863307 world languages:

Back page

We are all part of the same team

CHAPTER 49

OF THE QUEEN'S COACH, KNIGHTS, DIAMONDS, AND INVISIBILITY CLOAKS

An ornate black and golden coach from another age, exuding opulence and luxury, with fragments of Nelson's flagship victory, the Tower of London, Westminster Abbey and stately homes and palaces upon it, weighing 2.75 tons, more than 20 foot long and 10 foot high and with a team of six horses to pull drew up to the stadium.

It was a majestic work of art, every inch hand-made, wrought, carved, stitched and painted by blacksmiths, wheelwrights, bodymakers and heraldic artists. The carriage was heated with hydraulic stabilisers and had electric lighting with controls hidden in the arm rests, made from timber taken from the rails on the royal yacht Britannia. It had an aluminium body which was impervious to extremes of heat and humidity. Four coach lamps were spun in brass and the tops adorned with the royal crown. The glass panels were hand blown and cut by Edinburgh Crystal.

The door handles, made by a specialist in New Zealand were decorated with blue enamel and 27 diamonds each. The wheels, covered in pure gold. The interior lined with 20 yards of pale gold silk brocade. The design incorporated the rose, the flax, the thistle and the leek. The 23.5 carat English gold leaf used extensively on the coach comes from Birmingham gold beaters by royal appointment.

It was a time capsule of British history. A Britain where every man will do his duty, the Queen most of all. And that was why she was here.

A few ballboys opened a side entrance allowing her to ride in in full regalia and glory but she alighted as soon as the carriage drew onto the pitch. She removed her shoes and walked directly up to Gargantua and bowed before sitting opposite him.

The world looked on as both Queen and giant sat in silence. The world was silent.

After a fair amount of more silence, the Queen took off her garter, climbed up a ladder to the side of her coach and standing on the roof, handed it to Gargantua.

'I would like to thank you for the transformation of l'Undone. We owe you a huge debt of gratitude. We hereby give you the order of the garter for outstanding service'

Gargantua took the garter in one hand and smiled.

He handed her the Koh-i-Noor diamond and spoke:

'Once the Thames was calm, I took back the diamond and replaced the 'I' in its original position if not state. I told your guards I was only borrowing the diamond, as indeed are you, Maam. Remember you are not an independent state. Do not resist with separate visas and the like. You know, Maam, you are part of the common wealth, part of the globalisation. Still, it is up to you.

Perhaps, though, if the KohINoor does go back on display,

the diamond could remind each and every person of this moment.

Could these words be inscribed by it?:

'It's okay to have a diamond
as long as you don't think you own it.'

So saying, Dartagne and Zzorroa lifted the Z sword up to Gargantua who took it in his hand and relieved them of their duality.

He immediately raised it in the air and brought it down very gently indeed to the front of the Queen's heart, tracing the letter Z as he did so.

The Queen smiled as the pain in her aching feet dissolved and her sense of ageing melted away.

'Thank-you, even more potent than our homeopathic medicine' she replied.

Without further ado, Gargantua placed the cloaking device as outlined by Nicorovici and Milton in the Royal Society's scientific journal, over Dartagne and Zzorroa and himself.

Invisible, they departed, making a rapid few steps to place the swords of spiritual and temporal justice on Big Ben's clock. It started ticking again.

Another few steps led them to Stinkbomb which they cloaked as well. They were on their way.

For those of you who would like to know what became of them next, I would recommend volume two: 'What love is not'. For those of you who would like to know what became of the world, I would recommend a visit to l'Undone and a quick examination of the Koh-i-Noor diamond. Nothing is ever as it seems and everything is perfect as it is, we just can't always see it....

Acknowledgements, Gratitude, Credits and Permissions

To Andy Howe for the wonderful cartoon on the cover, thank you!
To Joanna Jones for her unfailing encouragement and trust,
To Sue and John Thornton for their heart,
To allmy bestfriends for that wonderful week-end and the spontaneous endorsement,
To John Hunt and his team for their vision and hard work,
To Martin, who believed in me at the start,
To Oliver Fry and Nic Barlow for the arty suggestions,
To Bernard Sharratt, James Essinger, Julia Vohralik (for synchronistic water), to Brian E. Mayne for the older versions (best present ever),
To Chris Vincent and his crew for the football chat,
To Graham Wright for Africa and India and Microsave finance,
The Lembrun family for the games, especially Ivan,
To John Lennon as writer of the unsurpassable 'Imagine' and to Lenono Music, the publisher, for their generous permission to use the lyrics and allow the joke to stay, thank you Yoko,
To Dr. Emoto: 'The Messages from Water' vol.2 by Hado Kyoiku Publishing Company for allowing me to quote his discoveries,
Melvyn Bragg for permission to quote from his programme on the heart,
A variety of Daily Telegraph journalists, including Sally F Pook and Nicole F Marting and especially the Sports section, thank you for your wonderful vocabulary,
Nicolae Nicorovici and Graeme Milton for the 'Cloaking Device',
To Paulo Coelho for the heart extract from 'The Alchemist', 1988, reprinted by permission of HarperCollins Publishers Ltd,
To Queen, Pink Floyd, and to all those who do not wish to be mentioned...
To Winston Churchill,
The Queen,
to the Queen's coach maker,
The guards at the Tower,
Rupert Sheldrake,
To all the famous people, trademarks, song, book and film titles I have quoted.

May it benefit!

O books
O is a symbol of the world, of oneness and unity. In different cultures it also means the "eye", symbolizing knowledge and insight, and in Old English it means "place of love or home". O books explores the many paths of understanding which different traditions have developed down the ages, particularly those today that express respect for the planet and all of life.

For more information on the full list of over 300 titles please visit our website
www.O-books.net

myspiritradio is an exciting web, internet, podcast and mobile phone global broadcast network for all those interested in teaching and learning in the fields of body, mind, spirit and self development. Listeners can hear the show online via computer or mobile phone, and even download their favourite shows to listen to on MP3 players whilst driving, working, or relaxing.

Feed your mind, change your life with O Books,
The O Books radio programme carries interviews with most authors, sharing their wisdom on life, the universe and everything...e mail questions and co-create the show with O Books and myspiritradio.

Just visit **www.myspiritradio.com** for more information.

SOME RECENT O BOOKS

The Barefoot Indian

Julia Heywood

Spiritual fiction, or not? Eternal wisdom is expressed in the context of modern day to day life, in a fresh, sensitive, intuitive, humorous and profoundly inspirational way.

1846940400 112pp **£9.99 $19.95**

Souls Don't Lie

A true story of past lives

Jenny Smedley

People often go on about past lives they believe they've had, but rarely has anyone explained so eloquently and succinctly the art and science of using past-life regression to heal the life you're living now - a fascinating and recommended read. **Barefoot Doctor**, healer and author.

1905047835 224pp **£11.99 $19.95**

Torn Clouds

A time-slip novel of reincarnation and romance, threaded through with the myths and magic of ancient Egypt.

Judy Hall

This is a great novel. It has suspense, drama, coincidence, and an extra helping of intrigue. I would recommend this literary marvel to anyone drawn to the magic, mystery and exotic elegance known as Egypt. **Planet Starz**

1903816807 400pp **£9.99 $14.95**

The Tree That Talked

Jenny Smedley

This is the story of an oak tree, from birth to death. Using the tree as our witness, we see many small moments in history-moments that rippled outward to affect the world. But the tree is more than a witness, it is connected to all the life around it. It, too, has its tragedies, its suffering, and times of renewal. After reading this, you won't think the same way about trees again.

1846940354 160pp **£10.99 $16.95**

Back to the Truth

5,000 years of Advaita

Dennis Waite

A wonderful book. Encyclopedic in nature, and destined to become a classic. **James Braha**

Absolutely brilliant...an ease of writing with a water-tight argument outlining the great universal truths. This book will become a modern classic. A milestone in the history of Advaita. Paula Marvelly

1905047614 500pp **£19.95 $29.95**

Beyond Photography

Encounters with orbs, angels and mysterious light forms

Katie Hall and John Pickering

The authors invite you to join them on a fascinating quest; a voyage of discovery into the nature of a phenomenon, manifestations of which are shown as being historical and global as well as contemporary and intently personal.

At journey's end you may find yourself a believer, a doubter or simply an intrigued wonderer... Whatever the outcome, the process of journeying

is likely prove provocative and stimulating and - as with the mysterious images fleetingly captured by the authors' cameras - inspiring and potentially enlightening. **Brian Sibley**, author and broadcaster.
1905047908 272pp 50 b/w photos +8pp colour insert **£12.99 $24.95**

Don't Get MAD Get Wise

Why no one ever makes you angry, ever!

Mike George

There is a journey we all need to make, from anger, to peace, to forgiveness. Anger always destroys, peace always restores, and forgiveness always heals. This explains the journey, the steps you can take to make it happen for you.
1905047827 160pp **£7.99 $14.95**

IF You Fall...

It's a new beginning

Karen Darke

Karen Darke's story is about the indomitability of spirit, from one of life's cruel vagaries of fortune to what is insight and inspiration. She has overcome the limitations of paralysis and discovered a life of challenge and adventure that many of us only dream about. It is all about the mind, the spirit and the desire that some of us find, but which all of us possess. **Joe Simpson**, mountaineer and author of *Touching the Void*
1905047886 240pp **£9.99 $19.95**